Advance Praise for
Enly and the Buskin' Blues

"A fast-paced, quirky caper with an authentic middle-grade voice."

—Alan Gratz, *New York Times* bestselling author

"Jennie Liu gently explores what gentrification can mean for communities, and in doing so she encourages readers who need to be seen as well as those who need to see. Enly is a fun, determined kid. Some of his choices made me cringe but more made me cheer him on, and I would stop to listen to him play the melodica anytime! I tip my hat to Liu—and put a tip in the hat for Enly!"

—Rebecca Petruck, author of *Boy Bites Bug*
and *Steering Toward Normal*

"In Jennie Liu's witty and wise new book, dreams come true with the help of family, friends, and a special community."

—Bobbie Pyron, author of *Lucky Strike*

Enly and the Buskin' Blues

Jennie Liu

✤ CAROLRHODA BOOKS
MINNEAPOLIS

Carolrhoda Books®
An imprint of Lerner Publishing Group, Inc.
241 First Avenue North
Minneapolis, MN 55401 USA

For reading levels and more information, look up this title at www.lernerbooks.com.

Cover and interior illustration by Michelle Jing Chan.

Main body text set in Bembo Std.
Typeface provided by Monotype Typography.

Library of Congress Cataloging-in-Publication Data

Names: Liu, Jennie, 1971– author.
Title: Enly and the buskin' blues / Jennie Liu.
Other titles: Enly and the busking blues
Description: Minneapolis, MN : Carolrhoda Books, [2023] | Audience: Ages 9–13. | Audience: Grades 4–6. | Summary: Hoping to earn money for band camp tuition, twelve-year-old Enly Wu Lewis starts busking, but his mission quickly turns into a series of misadventures that change how he sees his family, his dreams, and himself.
Identifiers: LCCN 2022005624 (print) | LCCN 2022005625 (ebook) | ISBN 9781728424569 | ISBN 9781728479378 (ebook)
Subjects: CYAC: Street musicians—Fiction. | Cities and towns—Fiction. | Racially mixed people—Fiction. | LCGFT: Fiction.
Classification: LCC PZ7.1.L5846 En 2023 (print) | LCC PZ7.1.L5846 (ebook) | DDC [Fic]—dc23

LC record available at https://lccn.loc.gov/2022005624
LC ebook record available at https://lccn.loc.gov/2022005625

Manufactured in the United States of America
1-49325-49441-6/28/2022

For my community.

1

"Enly! Enly! Wait for me!"

I was boarding the school bus at the end of the day and turned around on the steps to see my best friend, Pinky, jumping up and down at the back of the mob of kids waiting to get on. Her four thick coils of hair bounced around her head, the chunky beads on the ends of them clunking together as she waved a brightly colored piece of paper at me.

"I have to show you this!" she yelled over everyone's heads.

I tried to get off the bus, but the kids behind me were crowding up, blocking my way. Tia, the self-appointed bus monitor, stood towering over the steps. She leaned over and tapped me on the shoulder. "Uh-uh, buddy boy, where do you think you're going?" Her fingers went *snap, snap*, and then she pointed over her shoulder. "Get your jumbo bones up here and go sit next to Kenny."

It was on the tip of my tongue to say, *You can't tell me what to do*, but something about her whip-like bossiness and her already-developed chest intimidated me. I glanced over at Ms. Screws, who was sitting behind the steering wheel, sucking up a soda through a straw and looking at her phone. I knew she wouldn't be any help. She always just let Tia tell everyone what to do.

I tromped up the rest of the steps and down the aisle into the reek of armpit and cheap body spray, kicking aside discarded contraband snack bags to get to the middle of the bus. Kenny was one of the smallest kids in the whole school, whereas I was one of the biggest. My mom always said my father's white genes overtook the Chinese ones when it came to size. I was bulky and tall, which meant I had to sprawl my knees apart when I sat down so they wouldn't be jammed against the seat in front of me.

Tia turned around and snickered at Kenny and me. Unfortunately, puberty hadn't quite hit for either of us, and for some reason Tia thought it was hilarious to see an overgrown half-Chinese kid sitting next to the palest white-blond kid who was barely

2

visible over the seat. I rolled my eyes, but she just tossed her curly head and went back to dominating the bus riders.

"Hey, Enly," Kenny said, flashing a mouth full of braces at me.

"Hi, Kenny."

"I had the Chinese lunch in the cafeteria today." His voice was always high-pitched and squeaky.

I sighed, trying not to cross my eyes in weariness. Just because I was half Chinese, Kenny apparently thought he should share his Chinese food experience with me. But unlike Tia, he was at least trying to be nice. "Oh, really?"

"Yeah, it wasn't anything like Dragon Palace," he said. "The eggrolls tasted like sweaty feet."

I had never eaten at Dragon Palace and I wondered how he knew what sweaty feet tasted like, but I only grunted, "Hmph," because I was busy watching for Pinky and trying not to get clocked in the head by backpacks as the eighth graders squeezed past to the back of the bus.

Actually, I had kind of liked the school lunch. My mom might be Chinese, but she certainly wasn't making eggrolls and fried rice every night. Or ever. She didn't have time for all that chopping, folding, rolling, and frying. And she said that stuff was more American than anything.

Pinky eventually got on. Tia made her sit closer to the front, but she kept turning around to flap that piece of paper at me, pointing at it excitedly. I wondered what was so interesting.

I was thinking that it looked like some kind of pamphlet as Tia, done with lording over the rest of us, made her way to the back of the bus. She was hunched over her phone, not at all looking where she was going, when she tripped over my big old size nine, which was poking into the aisle. She didn't fall or anything, but that didn't stop her from lighting into me.

"Look what you did!" The bright orangey lipstick she wore made her mouth look like a stretchy rubber band as she screamed at me. "You almost made me drop my phone! Why are your gorilla feet sticking out in the aisle?"

"Sorry." I tried to pull my foot back under me. "I didn't do it on purpose."

The bus doors slapped shut, which was the signal that everyone's bottom had to be sitting. Tia kept walking toward her seat, muttering, "You better not be messing with me."

Meanwhile, Pinky was still trying to show me that piece of paper, but I couldn't even think about moving up until Tia got off at her stop. Only then was I able to dart into the vacant seat behind Pinky.

"Look at this!" Pinky said as she thrust the brochure at me. "Just look! It's the most amazing thing."

BAND AND JAM MUSIC SCHOOL
The quintessential music collaboration camp!

The words jumped out at me just before Pinky snatched the pamphlet back. She shook it open and started jabbing her finger at points of interest. "It's the most amazing music camp you ever heard of. They have all kinds of music lessons—not just classical. They teach you how to play in a band, any kind of band you want, even pop, rock, or rap!"

Pinky and I both played piano. Her lessons were classical, but she always wanted to play modern stuff. My repertoire was . . . well, let's just say even more limited.

"You even get to record an EP or make a video. And the best thing is that it's overnight for two weeks at a college in Atlanta!" She was still pointing at the photos, but she fluttered the paper so hard I couldn't see a thing. "Two weeks! You get to stay in the dorm and eat in the cafeteria, which means we can eat hot dogs and pizza every day if we want! And sodas! All the sodas we want for breakfast, lunch, and dinner. Take it! Take it!" She shoved the brochure at me again impatiently.

I finally got hold of it and leaned back in my seat so she wouldn't be tempted to grab it again before I could look at it for myself. On the cover, a teenager clutched a mic, eyes closed and mouth fully open as if he was really belting out a lyric. Stage lights sparkled all around him.

"It's absolutely perfect for both of us!" Pinky said. "My mom signed me up last night! You have to come."

My mouth twitched from side to side. I had never been to an overnight camp before. Usually Mom forced me to go to City Recreation Camp at the community center, where we had to make dry pasta necklaces and paint pet rocks.

"We can form our own band if we want. Mom said that I could finally start the guitar while I'm there." Pinky knelt backward on the seat but crouched down so Ms. Screws wouldn't notice. "We both can if you're ready to try something besides the piano." She screwed up her face. "And maybe you can break away from those—uh, how should I put it—those *chirpy* songs you play. I mean 'Danny Boy' and 'What a Friend We Have in Jesus' are catchy tunes and all, but dude, unless you want Danny and Jesus to be your only friends, something's gotta change."

"Ha, ha," I said. I'd been playing piano for only a couple of years. My lessons were with Ms. Maisie, who lived in the senior housing building where my mom used to work, but she wasn't a professional piano teacher or musician. And yes, I wanted to learn to read sheet music and to play "Bohemian Rhapsody" and the theme from *Star Wars*, but mostly Ms. Maisie taught me church songs and old show tunes she knew. She was kind of set in her ways. "Anyway, I want to stay with the piano," I murmured as I studied the brochure. The photographs of kids behind drum sets, keyboards, and sound equipment jumped out at me.

Form a band and develop practice skills with other musicians with similar experience and style.

Hone your skills with musical instruction from professionals and practice stage performance in concerts.

Discover the secrets of songwriting, recording, promotion.

"Wow, this does sound great!" I said. Lately, when I practiced at home on my keyboard, I'd been making up my own tunes. I could only play when I was by myself because my sixteen-year-old brother, Spencer, was always studying when he was at home, and I wasn't allowed to disturb him in our tiny apartment.

And Mom didn't really like to hear me play because it reminded her of Dad, who died when I was three. He'd been a musician and played in a band. She didn't talk really about him. Several years back when we were moving from our previous apartment into the one we lived in now, I'd seen her pulling out a big keyboard from a closet. I'd gotten really excited and started to drill her with questions—who did it belong to, why was it hidden away, could I play with it? Mom's face had gotten all trembly. She'd set the keyboard on the bed and rushed out of the room. When I'd plugged it in and started playing with it, Spencer had come in.

"Look what Mom found," I'd said. "Want to try it?"

Spencer had stared at it for a long moment before he came over and solemnly pressed a key. A low note hovered in the air. "That's Dad's keyboard," he said.

A cloudy memory had come back to me: standing at the keys while Dad played the upright piano we had in the old house. He would stop mid-song and wait for me to plink out a few notes before he picked it back up.

Spencer had glanced toward the other room where I could hear Mom and her friend moving things out to the truck she'd borrowed. "You'd better not play it while Mom's around. It just makes her sad."

Now, looking at the brochure, my heart began to patter. I could learn how to read music and to *really* play music.

I knew I had to do it. "I'll ask my mom as soon as I get home," I said.

2

For the rest of the bus ride, I thought about the video I'd found online a couple years back of Dad playing with his band at some bar. They were in the middle of a song and then the singer, guitarist, and drummer suddenly dropped off and Dad bore down on the keys, playing a fast and furious riff that he seemed to be improvising. An uptick of cheering and whistling from the audience could be heard in the background.

The video was grainy and wobbly as if it had been shot from an old-school camera. Whoever had taken it had gotten up on the stage because the video zoomed right up on Dad—first focusing on his fingers as they skipped all over the keys, then panning to his face when he flashed a big grin and winked at the camera.

If I went to camp, I could get pretty good. Maybe

not as good as Dad in such a short time, but good enough so I could work out how to play any song I wanted to learn and maybe write down the measures of the ones I made up so I wouldn't forget them. And then those songs could be played. By a band. Pinky's and my band.

I saw myself in a black leather jacket under the streaming stage lights, pounding out my songs on a full-size keyboard, surrounded by Pinky on guitar, a drummer, and singers. Our band name, The . . . The . . . well, whatever we decided to call ourselves, would be up in lights, and the audience would be screaming out our names along with the emcee: *Please welcome Enly Wu Lewis to the stage . . .*

I ran the three blocks from the bus stop to our apartment because I hoped to catch Mom before she left for her second job at the Golden Years Retirement Center, where she gave people showers, helped them get to the bathroom, and wiped their bottoms. During the day, Mom worked at the hospital as a nursing assistant pretty much doing the same thing, except the people in the hospital weren't necessarily old, and they used bedpans and got sponged down in bed rather than getting into the shower, according to Mom.

Mom was always so busy with her two jobs that I usually only saw her in the mornings before school and for a few minutes between her two shifts. She had to work so much because our little mountain town, Altamont, had gotten ridiculously expensive now that it'd been *found out* and everyone wanted to come here. We'd already had to move out of the apartment we used to rent because the owners wanted to make it a vacation rental. Mom said we were lucky to find a place in the same neighborhood near downtown, even though it was only a one-bedroom in an old Victorian house that'd been chopped up into a bunch of small apartments.

Spencer and I shared the bedroom while Mom slept on the green-and-red plaid fold-out couch in the living room. Sometimes she was too tired to move the coffee table and open up the bed, so she just slept on the couch with the quilt that usually hung over the back to hide the worn spots.

The living room and kitchen were pretty much one room, separated by a narrow counter. As soon as I burst in, I saw Mom's blue work-uniformed bottom sticking out of the fridge. She was bent over with her head inside, poking around, probably trying to drum up something for our dinner.

"Mom! I'm so glad you're still here." I skirted past the desk and the keyboard next to the door, then around the couch in the middle of the room to get to the kitchen. "I have to show you something."

Mom straightened up. "Is it your report card? It better be all A's." Her arm went around me with a half-squeeze before she began pulling plastic containers out of the fridge and placing them on the counter.

"No, Mom. Look at this camp." I held the brochure up to her face. "It's a music camp in Atlanta. You won't believe it, it's perfect for me!" I thrust the brochure at her.

She closed the fridge door before she took it out of my hand.

"They've got piano classes and lessons," I gushed, not waiting for her to read it. "They teach all kinds of things—not only how to play instruments, but music writing, theory, forming a band, recording. Just everything, everything related to music!"

Mom's head moved up and down slightly as she half-listened. Strands of her straight black hair slipped from her hair band and fell in her face. She opened the brochure and I watched her eyes move back and forth behind her glasses while she read. I bounced on my toes, trying not to interrupt her, but after a few moments I couldn't help myself.

"Pinky's already signed up. It's a two-week camp! Overnight! Music all day, and performances at night. That could be like ten hours of music a day!" I threw that in because I knew Mom valued hard work.

She flipped to the back of the brochure, her eyes skimming quickly over the page until they landed on something. "Pwah!" The noise was half gasp, half scoff, and she pushed the brochure back to me. "Forget it. It's not going to happen." She nudged me aside and started to open the containers, sniffing the contents and mixing leftovers together.

It was my turn to sputter. "But why not?"

Mom gave me her best dead-eye look and thunked me on the forehead with her finger before jabbing at the pamphlet in my hand. "Why don't you use your head a little bit more? Didn't you read that piece of paper all the way through to the back? Always rushing, rushing, rushing through everything. That's why you only get the ninety-fours and ninety-sixes on your tests."

I looked back at the pamphlet, turning it over to the back page. The *logistics* information that I hadn't bothered to study was there at the bottom. *Camp, room, meals, instrument if required . . . $2,800.00.*

$2,800! It was like a bomb dropped from a plane, whining through the air, and striking the ground with a thunderous boom.

"It's not that much," I said weakly, even though I knew it was an impossible amount. My entire savings amounted to sixty-eight dollars.

"Not that much?" Mom cocked her head back and puckered up her face like she smelled fermented bean curd. "Are you kidding me?"

"Pinky's going." I had to give it a try, even though I knew that it was hopeless.

Mom set the bowl down hard. Her eyebrows took on a dangerous slant and her nostrils flared. I could almost see smoke coming out of them. I knew I had said the wrong thing.

"Pinky's mom is a director of the YWCA and her dad works for the city. All you've got is me, working two low-paying jobs for this creaky apartment with footsteps over our heads, trying to save every penny." Mom leaned toward me with one hand on her hip and the other waving up at the ceiling. I just wanted to slink away, but I knew I couldn't until she was done.

"Their situation isn't our situation. And even if we had that kind of money, I sure wouldn't spend it on music camp! Music camp might be fine for Pinky and all those kids whose parents can throw away money letting them *explore their interests* and *follow their dreams*, but I have to focus on getting you and your brother through school, so you can get good jobs that get you off my payroll. Your brother has only one more year before he hits college. College! You know how much that's going to cost? If I had twenty-eight hundred dollars, it would go straight to the bank for that! I'm sorry, but the only place you're going this summer is City Rec Camp."

With my lips clamped together, I backed into the living room like a dog with its tail between its legs and sank down onto the couch. I couldn't believe I hadn't thought of the tuition. I probably wouldn't have gotten my hopes up if I had seen the price.

Of course we didn't have the money. All Mom ever worried about was money and how Spencer was going to get to college. Spencer was smart, really smart. Like the perfect student who loved school. And sure, he should go to college and be an engineer like he wanted, and like Mom wished she had done, but what if that wasn't for me? For heaven's sake, I was only twelve years old! Sure, I made pretty good grades without having to work too hard, but what was wrong with *exploring my interests*? What if it turned out that I was an untapped piano genius, or at least a really good musician like Dad? Didn't that matter?

The brochure was still in my hand. I set it on the coffee table and stared at the boy on the cover, wailing with his eyes closed like he was letting out everything inside him. I wondered what he was singing about. Probably how his mom didn't understand anything.

And I absolutely wasn't going to City Rec Camp again. Last year I'd been the oldest kid and bigger than half the staff. In the first week, one of the really young campers mistook me for a counselor and yanked on my shirt to tell me he'd had an accident. Unfortunately, he had first tried to stop the flow of pee as it was coming out, so his hands were soaked and I spent the rest of the day throwing up a little in my own mouth every time I caught a whiff of myself. I was not going back. No way.

Behind me in the kitchen, Mom continued to mix up the leftovers, dropping each emptied container into the sink with an angry clatter. Money was a touchy subject for her. I felt a little bad—not only because she worked so much and was always tired, but because she was also probably thinking about Dad.

I pictured Dad in his black T-shirt and jeans, his hair hanging over his eyes as he bent over the keyboard in the video. I often wondered how the heck he and Mom had ever gotten together.

I kept quiet, knowing that was the only way to let her cool down. By the time she finished making dinner, she was back to normal.

"Enly, did you do that English essay yet?"

I shook my head. "It's optional, Mom."

"Don't be lazy. You have to do it! What was the prompt?"

Describe your personal traits and how they affect your ambitions for the future. Ugh! Personal traits, ambitions, future. Who cared about that stuff? I just wanted to play my music.

"You'll have to write essays to get into college one day," Mom carried on without waiting for me to answer. She was rushing now, grabbing her keys and stuffing granola bars into her workbag. "Your teacher knows that, so she's offering the practice. Middle school is not too early to start thinking about

the future! Ask Spencer to help you if you get stuck."
She kissed me on the head and slipped on her shoes at
the door. "I cut some cantaloupe for you and put the
dinner in the fridge, so you can eat when you want.
Eat and wash the dishes before you go to piano."

I nodded and waited until she was gone before I
got up and looked at what she'd left in the fridge. My
eyes glazed past the fruit to the big glass bowl, which
held a liquidy mash of soup, rice, noodles, tofu, and
soggy vegetables. I scowled at it and shut the fridge
door. The pile of plastic and glass containers waited
for me in the sink. I ignored them and decided that
when Spencer got home from his afterschool job I'd
tell him Mom said for him to wash them.

I put two cups of water in a pot on the stove to
boil, opened the cabinet under the sink, and reached
in the back where Mom kept her secret stash of
instant ramen hidden behind the cleaning supplies.
Mom never let us eat instant noodles. She grew up
snacking on them, until Grandma read in the Chinese newspaper that two students died from having
them three times a day, every meal. They weren't
good for us, Mom said, but whenever we went to the
Asian grocery store and she saw the whole aisle full
of those crinkly packets, she couldn't resist. I always

went to look at the live crabs and dead fish on ice to give her time to slip a few packs under the other groceries in the cart.

When the three minutes of boiling time were almost up, I cracked an egg, whipped it in a bowl, dropped it into the ramen, and stirred it gently with chopsticks. The egg cooked in tasty shreds as I added the seasoning and oil packets. I poured it all into a bowl and took it to the coffee table and sat on the floor, waiting for it to cool enough to eat.

My eye fell on the Band and Jam pamphlet, and I studied it all over again. I knew I should just forget about it, but I was sure there had to be a way. While I slurped up the noodles, I thought and thought.

Would Grandma pay? Probably not. She was Chinese and didn't believe being a musician was a reliable career. She'd never been happy that Mom didn't finish college and that Dad had died doing musician things. According to Spencer, Grandma used to tell Mom that Dad was wasting his time running around at night playing music when he should be concentrating on moving up in his day job. She blamed the music for Dad's death since he was on his way home from a gig when he was killed in a car accident.

Yeah, Grandma definitely was out. Even if she could cough up twenty-eight hundred dollars, she'd probably rather invest it in Spencer, just like Mom.

Could I get a job? I figured you had to be sixteen to get a real job, but sometimes I was the backup cat sitter for our neighbor Marybeth when she went out of town. I only got to do it if her regular cat sitter wasn't available, but it was worth checking to see if she had any trips planned.

I did a quick calculation in my head. If Marybeth was gone every day between now and the end of July, and she paid me five dollars a day, that would still only be about six hundred dollars. Still, that would be a good chunk of the fee. I decided to check with her later this evening, even though it was a long shot that both she and her regular cat sitter were going away for four months.

Meanwhile, it was time for my piano lesson.

3

I crossed the overpass into downtown and walked the two blocks to the Olmstead Apartments, where my mom used to work as an activities coordinator. The building was an old hotel that had been converted to apartments for seniors. Affordable housing, Mom said, for elderly people who didn't have a lot of money. Unfortunately, this also meant that Mom's job eventually got eliminated.

When Mom worked there, she used to decorate the bulletin boards and organize potlucks, game nights, and musical entertainment. I had to hang out there after school, so I got to know some of the residents, including Ms. Maisie, who started giving me piano lessons in exchange for my running errands for her because she couldn't walk very far. She'd been playing ever since she was a kid herself, and she could still pound out the music even though her eyes were bad.

When I got to the Olmstead, Ms. Maisie was already parked by the upright piano on the far side of the activity room, perched on the seat of her four-wheel walker with her elbows resting on the handles. I crossed the room, weaving around all the tables and chairs. There were a few residents at the tables, reading newspapers or playing Candy Crush on their tablets. One woman was knitting.

As I slid onto the bench, Ms. Maisie startled. "Enly! You surprised me."

"Sorry, Ms. Maisie," I said.

"You usually bound in here with your sneakers slapping the linoleum so hard that I can hear you as soon as you enter the building! You're not sick, are you?" Her wrinkled face wrinkled even more under her stiff cloud of burgundy hair, which always made me hungry for grape cotton candy—if there was such a thing. The hair was dyed. I knew this, not only because the color was too purply-red to be a natural shade and Ms. Maisie was at least eighty years old, but also because I picked up the box of dye from the drugstore for her every month.

"Oh, no, I'm fine. I just had some bad news," I told her.

Ms. Maisie leaned in and peered at me, waiting for me to say more. I explained about the music camp.

"Oh dear!" She patted my arm. "I so wish I could do something to help you. You're such a hardworking little—well, big-little—musician. I can tell you always practice everything I give you."

I noticed she didn't say *talented musician*, but I smiled at her. "Well, you do help me by giving me these lessons."

"I know, sweetie. And you help me. Don't give up on the camp just yet. Something may happen to make it work out for you." Her fingers reached up and fluffed her hair, which didn't actually move. "Now, Enly, are you ready to learn a new song?"

I bobbed my head eagerly. I had hinted to Ms. Maisie last week that I wanted to learn something new, maybe something a bit more current. I had played "The Imperial March" from *Star Wars* for her several times on the computer in the activity room, thinking that maybe she could learn the song and teach it to me. She had been plinking out a few bars of it when I left her last time.

"I have a surprise for you!" She clambered up from her walker. Her joints creaked as she turned around and flipped up the seat to reach into the basket beneath it. Then she slowly turned around and handed me a book of music. "Gerald from the second floor found this in the used bookstore over on Lexington Street. You know, that bin where they have old records and music books."

I looked at the title. *The Broadway Collection: Easy Piano Series.*

Luckily Ms. Maisie was so thrilled with the book that she didn't see the horrified grimace I couldn't hold back. My heart sank as she opened it in my hands and turned the pages to show me the titles. "The Yankee Doodle Boy," "I Feel Pretty," "Put on a Happy Face."

I recognized some of the songs from old movies my mom made me watch as part of what she called my classic film education, which was really just Mom wanting to revisit the musicals she liked to watch.

"Now, I was thinking maybe we could start with 'Give My Regards to Broadway' or 'There's No Business Like Show Business,'" she said.

I swallowed a lump in my throat and tried to smile. Maybe because Ms. Maisie was so old, she considered these songs to be new. But I couldn't hurt her feelings, so I said, "Okay. Let's do 'There's No Business Like Show Business.'"

Ms. Maisie clapped her hands and her eyes got all bright. She seemed like she'd gotten a shot of vitamins as she moved onto the bench beside me, nudged me to scoot over, and began to bang out the song. She played it all the way through, singing the lyrics in her high, tinkling voice, before she began to break it down for me, squinting at the sheet music.

We worked on the song for the rest of the session and darn if it didn't get stuck in my head. Afterward, I caught myself singing the lyrics under my breath as I headed down to Mountain Discount Pharmacy to pick up a few things for Ms. Maisie. I crumpled up my face trying to squeeze the tune out of my head. At this rate, if I only learned show tunes, I'd never get to be Enly the Really Awesome Piano Player, or whatever my stage name or band name would be.

On Haywood Street, a few tourists were standing close to a life-sized bronze lady in a long, old-fashioned dress. Downtown Altamont had a few bronze statues of fiddle players, old-time dancers, and a giant iron, but this lady wasn't really a statue. She was a real woman with every inch of her hair, skin, and clothes covered in metallic paint. Even the small basket of acorns she held, the box she stood on, and the tall pot she had placed against the base for tips were painted. But people didn't seem to realize that she was a street performer. The statue stood stock-still waiting for someone to toss money into her pot before she came alive, but the group ignored her as they studied a big upright map of the downtown area.

A boy with the group—he looked about three years old—didn't really notice the statue either, but he wandered over to her tip pot. When he leaned over to look inside it, his face lit up like he'd just found a treasure. He reached into the pot.

I didn't see the statue move, because that's how the really good ones work, but in the next second, a painted acorn bounced off the boy's shoulder. His hand flew up to rub the spot, and he swiveled around trying to figure out what had just happened. He glanced up at the sky, the buildings, even at me. I just shrugged.

The living statue stayed frozen with a pleasant look on her face. Just a few moments earlier both hands had been grasping the basket. Now, she had an acorn in the fingertips of one hand, almost like she was ready to chuck it at someone. I watched her carefully this time as the clueless little boy went back to dipping his hand into her pot, but instead of lobbing the acorn at him, I heard her growl in a low voice, "Back off, buddy."

I couldn't help but smother a laugh as the boy ran over to his dad and clutched his leg. He stared at the statue, completely bewildered.

At the pharmacy, I picked up Ms. Maisie's hair dye, aerosol hair spray, three cans of tuna fish, a jar of peanut butter, and a loaf of white bread. I reached for a box of Twinkies but then remembered that Ms. Maisie had said to skip them along with the gherkins and string cheese today. Ms. Maisie was on a fixed income, so on hair coloring weeks she had to cut back on other treats. It seemed kind of sad, but she said that was the price of beauty.

Back outside, music was coming from across the street near Altamont Books and News. There was a crowd of people waiting to get inside the store. A jazzy number played over them, and a few people swayed and bobbed their heads. They didn't seem to mind waiting. I crossed over and saw a big poster in the bookstore window. It said that a local chef was signing her new book today; that was probably what everyone was in line for. Saxophone Joe was parked outside the store in his power wheelchair, blaring away on his saxophone.

I knew Saxophone Joe lived at the Olmstead, but I hardly ever saw him there. He didn't hang out in the activity room or linger outside the building smoking and enjoying the sun like some of the residents. His left pant leg was folded over and pinned at his thigh because he didn't have any leg below his knee. Ms. Maisie said he was a war veteran and had played with some famous blues and jazz bands in his day. She also thought he was kind of a grump.

This wasn't necessarily because he'd lost his leg, but more likely because he never got enough sleep. He played his saxophone outside the civic center or the baseball stadium, staying up late to catch the audience coming and going from the events. Ms. Maisie said he'd been playing the saxophone on the sidewalks of Altamont for years and years, since way before the town started showing up on the Best Places to Live and Best Places to Visit lists—since before street performing and busking became a *thing* here. She said now that Altamont had become such a popular tourist destination, Saxophone Joe probably made some pretty good money.

Pretty good money.

I craned my neck to look at the shoebox Saxophone Joe had placed on the sidewalk near his wheelchair. It was full of cash. There was so much that the bills almost overflowed the sides of the box. I thought of that tall pot the living statue kept at her base. I hadn't seen how much money was in it, but that boy's face had certainly glowed at the sight.

My heart began to thump and thump, because I suddenly knew how I was going to get the money for Band and Jam.

4

The next day, I was late coming out of Spanish because Profa Rosa had brought her accordion to school to play for us, and I wanted to see it up close after everyone else left the classroom. She let me strap it on. It was heavy. I almost tottered over for a second, but it fit pretty well since I was just about as tall as Profa Rosa. Once I started playing the keys and pushing the bellows and buttons, it was like patting my head and rubbing my stomach at the same time. If I'd had more time, I would've nailed it, but I wanted to find Pinky and see if she would help me with my plan.

When I got to the cafeteria, the clatter and chaos of lunch was in full swing. I scanned for Pinky and saw she was already eating with a bunch of girls. She spotted me at the same moment and waved me over.

I hadn't gotten my lunch yet, but since the line snaked long—pizza dippers day—I hustled over to her table. Pinky scooted the girls over so I could squeeze onto the end of the bench.

"Did you tell your mom about Band and Jam?" She took a big bite of her sandwich, red jelly on wheat, and chewed with her mouth open. Although it looked gruesome, the smell of the jelly made my stomach growl.

"Yeah. It costs too much for us." I shrugged like it didn't matter.

"Oh." Pinky obviously hadn't thought about the cost either. I figured she didn't have to.

"But I still want to go," I said. "And I have an idea to make the money for the tuition."

"Lemonade stand?" Pinky wrinkled her nose.

I shook my head. "Nah." We had done a couple of lemonade stands in the past, but usually in the middle of summer when it got really hot. Besides, we were too old for that. "Better. Busking!"

Pinky stared at me, waiting for more information.

"You know, like all those street performers who play downtown on the sidewalks! I can play my keyboard and put out a hat for tips."

Pinky's eyes got big and her mouth opened wide,

so I could tell she thought it was a great idea. The food was gone from her mouth, but I could smell that the jelly had been strawberry.

"I know, right?" I said. "I saw that guy Saxophone Joe yesterday, and he must've had twenty or thirty dollars in his tip box."

"Thirty dollars in one day?"

"Yeah, and it was only around four-thirty. I'll bet his box gets filled up a couple times when he stays out there for a few hours." I had wondered about this last night when I went to bed and had done all kinds of calculations in my head.

"You've got months and months before the camp," Pinky said, "You could make the tuition, easy."

"I want to get started after school. Today! I can carry my keyboard, but I need help to bring a big box or something to set it on and a stepstool for me to sit on. Can you come with me this afternoon?"

Pinky's face fell. "You know my mom doesn't like me to go downtown by myself."

"You wouldn't be by yourself," I said. "I'll be with you."

She made a face. "Same difference to her."

Our downtown was small, probably about seven or eight blocks in each direction, in a valley

33

surrounded by hills and mountains, but Pinky's mom still worried about all kinds of stuff like germy park benches, stray dogs, and *people experiencing homelessness*. She said it that way because she was into something called Asset-Based Thinking for Social Justice, which was about recognizing the value of every person. Apparently there were all kinds of reasons people might become homeless that were beyond their control, like addiction, mental illness, and lack of affordable housing and healthcare.

Pinky and I got what she was saying, but what we didn't get was why she was scared for Pinky to go downtown, especially if we were supposed to focus on people's potential and dignity and whatnot. I'd been going all over our small downtown by myself the last couple of years—to piano, errands, the library, the ice cream shop where Spencer worked— and no one had ever bothered me.

"But I can't carry everything by myself. I really need help."

Pinky shrugged. "More than anyone, you know how moms can be."

I sighed. That was certainly the truth. "We'll think of something." Maybe I could talk to her mom. She'd set that no-crossing-the-overpass-into-downtown rule for Pinky years ago, but we were in middle school now.

Luckily, the solution came to me in social studies when Mr. Davis assigned us to take photos of our neighborhood over the weekend. We had been studying local government and now we were starting a unit called Studying Our Community. I just knew that Pinky's mom would want her to complete her assignment to the best of her ability.

On the bus that afternoon, after Tia got off, I scooted next to Pinky and explained my plan. We'd tell her mom we were going to work together on the community project, starting this very afternoon.

"I consider downtown a big part of my neighborhood." I elbowed her. "Nudge, nudge, know what I mean?"

She mouthed a big *O* as she got my meaning. We would just say *neighborhood* and leave out the part about crossing the overpass into downtown.

Pinky called her mom at work and told her all about the project, throwing in some of the things we were supposed to be learning about: civics, awareness of surroundings, mapping hazards, safe community, social responsibility, gentrification. She laid it on thick, and it worked. Her mom said she thought it sounded like a wonderful assignment dealing with some very important issues.

But we only got as far as my apartment before my plan to make Band and Jam money crumbled again.

At home, my keyboard sat on two side-by-side chairs in the living room. I was emptying out a couple of milk crates filled with some old toys that seemed like they would make a good portable stand for the keyboard when Pinky called out from the living room.

"Uh, Enly. There's a little bit of a problem here."

"What is it?" I came out of the bedroom with the two plastic crates.

"This." She held up the keyboard's plug-in cord and swung it back and forth.

I groaned. I'd forgotten about the keyboard being electronic. That meant it had to be plugged in. "Crap!" I dropped the crates and flopped down onto the couch.

Pinky sat down beside me and put her feet up on the coffee table. "Can we use batteries?"

I shook my head. The keyboard didn't take batteries. And even if I had a giant extension cord, I didn't think any business owners would agree to let me connect my keyboard to an indoor electrical outlet. That would probably be a safety hazard.

The Band and Jam brochure was on the table under her foot. I grabbed it and smoothed it out where it had been wrinkled from all the handling.

"This sure would be easier if I played the guitar," I said.

"But the piano's your thing, right?"

"Yep." I glanced over to the heavy keyboard.

"It's too bad you don't have an accordion like Profa Rosa," Pinky said. "Did you have Spanish today?"

"Yup. She let me play it for a second. It was pretty cool. Kinda hard, but I bet I could learn it." I air-played the accordion, my right hand fingering the keys and the left hand pushing and pulling the bellows, and an idea began to wheeze into my head. "Hey, how much do you think those things cost?"

Pinky turned up her palms. "I have no idea."

"I've got sixty-eight dollars from Chinese New Year and cat sitting," I said, sitting up on the edge of the couch.

Pinky scooted forward too, starting to catch my drift. "You know, my dad says sometimes you have to spend money to make money!"

"But where would I get an accordion?" I wondered.

"Online?" Pinky suggested.

"Sure, but my mom would have to help me because I'd have to use a credit card." I'd have to explain the whole plan to her, and she probably wouldn't be on board.

Pinky tried again. "Is there a music store any-where downtown?"

That was a more promising idea. It would be easier just to pay for an accordion myself and skip the chance of Mom squashing the plan.

We both racked our brains.

"I feel like I've seen a bunch of guitars in a store window across from the pizza place on O'Henry Avenue with the big outdoor patio," I said.

"I know what you're talking about! I saw it when we ate over there one time. My dad said it's a pawnshop. People take stuff there to sell or get loans on it."

"Let's go!" I ran to my room and grabbed my wallet from under my mattress.

We were nearly out the door when Pinky reminded me to bring my phone—my mom's old one that didn't have service but was still good for pictures—so we could do our assignment. We took a few photos as we headed to the pawnshop.

Lichtenberger's Pawn and Loan, established 1903, Altamont's Longest-Running Store was printed on the red sign above the awning. It was squeezed between an olive oil tasting room, whatever that was, and a sushi restaurant. The shop windows on either side of the door were filled with guitars, banjos, even ukuleles.

"I don't see any accordions," I said.

Pinky peered through the glass door. "Let's go inside. There are more instruments in there."

The bell on the door tinkled as we entered. The store was long and narrow. Glass cases filled with jewelry, knives, and baseball cards lined both sides of the room. Instruments hung on racks or were laid on shelves against the walls. Televisions, electronics, old record players and typewriters, and even more instruments were displayed in the center along the length of the store. Pinky and I edged along slowly, our eyes running over everything. There was so much to look at. "Maybe you can get your electric guitar here," I said to Pinky.

"Hey." A man came out from the back. His head was smooth and shiny-pink, but he wasn't old like you'd expect a bald person to be. I guessed he shaved it. His tag said *Buck Lichtenberger, Proprietor.*

When he saw us he looked surprised and glanced at the door as if expecting our parents to be right behind us. "Something I can help you with?"

"Do you have any accordions?" I asked.

"Hmm. That's not the usual request, but you know what, I think I actually do."

He went behind the glass counters and ducked down to the cabinets under the shelves, then pulled out a big case. When he opened it, I saw the accordion inside: cherry red, the black and white keys looking clean and bright on the side.

"Ever play one of these?" Mr. Lichtenberger asked.

"A little." I *had* played for five minutes with Profa Rosa, after all.

"You want to try it?" He started to pull it out.

"How much is it?" I asked.

"This here fine instrument will cost you"—he searched around for the tag on the case—"three hundred and twenty dollars."

Ugh. That took the wind out of me. "I guess I don't need to try it out after all."

"A little too much?" Mr. Lichtenberger's face crimped up sympathetically.

"I only have sixty-eight dollars."

"So much for busking," Pinky sighed.

"Busking? Is that what you're aiming to do?" Mr. Lichtenberger asked. Without waiting for an answer, he packed up the accordion and went back to the cabinet. "I'll tell you what, I've got just what you need."

He rummaged around, then brought up a much smaller cloth case. He unzipped it and drew out a small keyboard with both black and white keys, about the length of my forearm with a flexible tube attached. "Ever seen one of these?"

Pinky and I both shook our heads.

"It's called a melodica," he said.

I plunked one of the keys but nothing happened.

"You have to blow into the tube at the same time. Like this." He put the tube between his lips and blew while his fingers tapped on the keyboard. The most wonderful sound came out. It sounded just like the accordion. Or was it like a harmonica? Maybe a little of both.

"It's really a wind instrument," Mr. Lichtenberger explained. "But there's a lot you can do with this. You can play it on a table, on your lap, or even holding it." He detached the long tube and replaced it with a short, hard mouthpiece, then brought the instrument up to his mouth with one hand. He began to play a jazz tune, holding the melodica like a saxophone, swaying and tilting the instrument in the air like I had seen Saxophone Joe do when he really got a tune going.

I pictured myself on the sidewalk, outside Supreme Cream or the library, jamming with this thing as the dollars rained down on me. And later in the summer, Pinky and I would be at Band and Jam under the colored stage lights, tearing it up with our band. Maybe I'd even jump up from the piano and play the melodica for a song or two.

Mr. Lichtenberger finished playing and wiped the mouthpiece with a tissue. He held the melodica out to me. "Here, try it."

Pinky and I looked at each other. We were both thinking of the germs that her mom was always carrying on about. She gave a tiny shake of her head.

"Uh, that's okay, I don't need to try it," I said.

Mr. Lichtenberger looked confused. "Why not?"

I couldn't help but glance at the tissue. I'm not a germophobe or anything, but still.

"Oh, I get it." He chuckled and rummaged in a drawer for something that he sprayed on the mouthpiece before wiping it again with a clean tissue. "How about that?"

I grinned and took the melodica, positioning it like he had, before I blew and plinked out a few notes. The sound that came out was harsh and blatty, like a baby goat crying for its mama.

Pinky put her fingers in her ears.

"Try to blow more gently," Mr. Lichtenberger advised.

"Wait, I got to get a picture of this!" Pinky pulled out her phone.

I brought the melodica up to my mouth again, not blowing so hard, and played a few bars of the first thing that came to mind, which was "There's No Business Like Show Business." I ran out of breath pretty quick.

"It takes a bit of practice, but it's portable. And I'll bet it's in your price range." Mr. Lichtenberger fumbled for the tag hanging on the carrying bag. "Forty-eight dollars. Plus tax, of course."

I looked at Pinky. She nodded, urging me on.

"I'll take it!"

5

With my new instrument in its case, slung across my back by its strap, Pinky and I headed up Walnut Street back to Haywood Avenue. I wanted to show the melodica to Ms. Maisie, and because the Olmstead residents often hung around outside the building, I thought they would be a perfect audience for my first performance.

Ms. Maisie was sitting on her walker outside the apartment complex. A few of the other folk were hanging out with her on the benches and in their wheelchairs. A bunch of pigeons pecked at some breadcrumbs tossed to them by a lady on an electric scooter—not the standing, two-wheel ones that let you zip around town, but the kind with a cushy swivel seat that old people use.

"Ms. Maisie! Look at this!" I unzipped the case

and showed her the melodica.

"Oh my! I haven't seen one of those things in years!" Ms. Maisie exclaimed.

"What is it? A keyboard?" the lady feeding the pigeons said.

"No. See that tube? It's a . . . what's it called, Enly?" Ms. Maisie asked.

"A melodica," I said. "I just bought it at the pawnshop. For busking, to make money for music camp."

"That's wonderful! I was sure you would think of something." Ms. Maisie clasped her hands together. "Why don't you play something for us?"

I pulled out the melodica and put it up to my mouth. With the first note, which came out loud and wonky, the pigeons scattered into the air like someone had thrown a handful of gravel at them. Ms. Maisie flinched a little but gave me an encouraging smile.

"Give me your phone, Enly. I'll take some photos of you so you'll have them for your assignment," Pinky said.

I handed her my phone and started playing again, trying not to blow too hard. I fingered out "Tomorrow," which Ms. Maisie had told me came from a musical called *Annie*. It was harder than I expected— using only one hand and trying to control the flow of air so I didn't run out of breath too quickly. Unfortunately, I had to break a few times in the middle of the song before I got to the end, but when I did finish, everyone clapped like I had done a good job.

Pinky had backed up several yards and taken a few shots of me. Now she rushed over and arranged the melodica's soft zippered case at my feet. "For tips!" she said to the residents.

One of the residents leaning against the wall patted at his pockets but didn't come up with anything. Someone else threw a few coins into the case.

"Oh, goodness," Ms. Maisie said, "you know, everyone here is mostly on fixed incomes. We're not going to be your best customers, Enly. You ought to plant yourself near some of the fancy boutiques and restaurants. Get some of that tourist money. Don't you think, Joe?" Ms. Maisie waved at someone behind me.

It was Saxophone Joe, powering himself along the sidewalk toward the Olmstead in his motorized wheelchair. As he passed us, he shook his head and put his hand up near his ear. I figured it was part greeting and part wave of dismissal, because he didn't answer and just went into the building.

Ms. Maisie grunted a *hmph*.

"I think that's a great idea!" I said. "How do you think I sound?"

"A little more practice certainly won't hurt," Ms. Maisie admitted. "You know what I think about practicing."

"I'll practice while I busk! Saves time." And I didn't want to lose out on any tips. "Let's go, Pinky."

We decided to run over to Supreme Cream, where Spencer worked after school. I would've gone inside to show him my new instrument, but I could see through the window that people were lined up while he scuttled behind the freezers with his ice-cream scoop. He wouldn't appreciate a distraction.

On the sidewalk bench near the shop, a family with two toddlers sat eating cones. "A perfect captive audience," Pinky declared and steered me in front of the Supreme Cream window. She was right—this was my chance.

Strangely, though, my stomach began to flip-flop. The two little boys' eyes were on me as I pulled out the melodica. Their cones dripped onto the side-walk as they gawked. This wasn't quite the same as playing for the Olmstead crowd.

Pinky nudged me, so I started to play. Maybe the music came out sort of cranky and loud, because one of the boys dropped his cone and put his hands up to his ears. He started to bawl and his parents jumped up from the bench. I kept playing, determined to finish a song without stopping for breath, but I knew it was rough.

Customers coming out of the Supreme Cream were grimacing at me. The sidewalk wasn't very wide here and people were trying to pass me. Someone nearly tripped on my case.

The next thing I knew, Spencer was outside, scowling behind his thick glasses. "What are you doing out here?" he demanded.

I finished and huffed for breath. "Look!" I held up the melodica. "I just bought this. I'm busking. To make money for music camp."

"Well, you can't do it here! You sound horrible. You're disturbing the peace and causing an obstruction on the sidewalk. Besides, don't you need a permit or something? Now beat it before the manager comes out." He went back inside.

Pinky grunted in disapproval. "How rude!"

That was Spencer. He wasn't really mean, just protective of his work.

"Does he ever give you free ice cream?" Pinky asked, gazing through the window hopefully.

"No. He gets a free pint every week, but he never shares it with me. Says he's underpaid and that's his only additional compensation."

Pinky sniffed. Then her face turned worried. "What about the permit he mentioned? Do you think he's serious about that?"

I shrugged. I was more bothered by what he'd said about me sounding horrible. Even though Spencer didn't share his ice cream, he usually told the truth. I thought about the little kid putting his hands up to his ears and the screwed-up faces of the people passing by.

We called it a day. I trudged home and practiced all evening.

6

Pinky took dance lessons Saturday mornings, so the next day, I decided to go out on my own. I tried to slip out before Mom started bugging me about working on my extra-credit essay, but the darn door always stuck in the morning because of the humidity. I had to jerk it hard to get it to open. The scrape and squeak of wood made Mom lift her head from the pillow she was hugging under her flowery comforter. She hadn't bothered to unfold the sleeper again.

"Where are you going?" she mumbled before her eyes were really even open.

"Out. Just downtown."

She sat up, rubbing the crusts out of her eyes and reaching for her glasses at the same time.

"Have you eaten?"

"I had a cheese sandwich."

"Cold?" She squinted at me and frowned as she evaluated the sustenance content of the meal. For some reason, she thought warm cheese toast had more value than just having it cold.

"Yeah, Mom. It was fine. Don't worry. I have to go." I knew her next question was going to be if I had eaten any fruit, so I started out the door.

"Wait! What's that bag you're carrying?"

The melodica in its case was slung on my shoulder. "It's an instrument. A melodica. I bought it yesterday." Mom had gotten home late last night and had popped her head into the bedroom just after I turned off my reading lamp, so I hadn't had a chance to tell her about it. "I'm going to use it to busk."

She didn't say anything for a very long moment, but I could practically read her mind through the sequence of expressions that crossed her face. First her mouth showed a little surprise. Then her forehead crinkled with disapproval about my hanging out on the streets, getting too entranced with music, and suspicion as to why I wanted to busk.

But she didn't have to ask why, because the answer was obvious. Money. This she could understand, and her lips began pinching and twitching as she tried to work out whether my attempt to make money from busking was a good thing ($$$!) or a bad thing (might encourage me to think that I could make a living this way ☹).

I wasn't about to explain what I planned to do with the money I earned, because of course she wouldn't be happy about that. I wondered if Mom and Dad had ever had arguments about his chasing his dream. Had she ever told him to forget about music and nagged him to just concentrate on his day job like she now nagged me about school? Had he begged her to be supportive?

Spencer and I had a picture in our room of a much younger Mom and Dad at night with their arms around each other. They were standing near a van with instruments unloaded on a sidewalk, so I imagined Dad had been getting ready to play somewhere. Mom was dressed up in a tight black mini-dress and she looked happy, so I liked to think she'd believed in him, even if it was too hard for her to see me doing the same thing.

But right now, I certainly didn't want to get drawn into a conversation about my future, so I took advantage of her mixed-up-feelings moment and said, "I've got to go, Mom. Have to get there early to get a good spot!" I stepped out and started to shut the door behind me.

"Wait! Wait!" Mom called out again.

I sighed and really fought not to roll my eyes, but I kept my hand on the knob.

Mom shot up from the couch, ran to the kitchen, and then came to the door. She thrust two apples at me, kissed me on the head, and thankfully said nothing more about the busking.

After I crossed the overpass bridge, I stopped at the metal newspaper and free magazine boxes lined up in front of the library. There was one box on the end with a glass door framed in wood that opened to the side. It was like a Little Free Library, but instead of books, it was filled with granola bars, pop-top cans of soup, and bottles of water meant for people experiencing homelessness. I opened up the little pantry and set the two apples inside. An unhoused person could probably use, and might want, the fruit more than I did.

Downtown was still pretty quiet. I set up shop outside Altamont Books and News, which I knew was a hot spot for buskers. The cheese sandwich I had wolfed down for breakfast churned in my stomach. Nerves—I guess every musician must get them before a show. I attached the tube mouthpiece to the instrument, wishing Pinky were here with me, but I knew I didn't have a moment to lose if I was going to make $2,800 in the next few months.

I began to play through all the songs Ms. Maisie had taught me. I sounded better than yesterday, but I still missed notes and had to draw in breath a lot of times, which made the music heave and haw.

People came out of the bookstore with their coffee, and others trickled by, but no one really stopped to listen. It was only about 10:30 in the morning, so there wasn't a whole lot of foot traffic like in the afternoon. A few people did drop some change, though.

At one point, a group of older boys passed by really close, laughing and snickering at me. My face got hot, and not just because the sun was beating down on me. But I kept playing.

Only after they were way down the block did I notice that one of them had dropped a half-eaten hoagie in my case. The wrapper was open, and the salami and tomato were sliding out of the bread. Pepperoncini and jalapeños—which I loved—poked out too, but of course I wasn't about to eat it.

Fuming, I picked up the sandwich and threw it

in the direction of the guys. They were way too far to catch it in the back. Really, I wouldn't have tried to hit them anyway because I didn't want them turning around and messing with me even more. At least the pigeons would get something out of it.

The hoagie had left a few seeds from the bread in my instrument bag. I picked out the coins and shook the case, fully discouraged now. The hooting and cheering of the audience at Dad's gig in the YouTube video jumped into my head. I wondered if he had sucked this bad when he first started out. Surely no one ever chucked a sandwich at him, I thought as I counted out the change.

Sixty-seven cents. I'd been out there at least half an hour and all I had was sixty-seven cents. Pitiful. That was a long way from $2,800. I thought about the fifty-one dollars and thirty cents I had spent on this thing. What a ridiculous idea, and even with today's tips I was still fifty dollars and sixty-three cents further from my goal. I decided to give it up and go check with Marybeth about cat sitting.

As I was putting the melodica back into its case, the back of my neck prickled. I looked up to see Saxophone Joe in his power wheelchair, parked across the street near the pharmacy, watching me.

When he saw me looking at him, he started swinging his head from side to side. Then he took up the knob at the end of his wheelchair's armrest and whizzed himself across the street in my direction.

At first I got edgy, afraid he was coming to scold me for taking his busking spot. But then I noticed that he only had a white pharmacy bag in his lap. His saxophone wasn't with him.

He pulled up next to me. "What's your name?" he asked.

"Enly."

"You trying to make some money?"

I nodded.

"Where'd you get that thing?" He gestured at my case.

"Lichtenberger's Pawn and Loan."

"My buddy Buck sold that to you?"

I nodded again.

"Ain't that called a melodica?" Saxophone Joe asked.

"Yes," I said.

"Yeah. Stevie Wonder played one of them a couple of times. You know any Stevie Wonder songs?"

I shook my head.

"Let me hear you play something."

I took the melodica back out and started playing "Tomorrow." Saxophone Joe's face cramped up when the sound came out too loud, and he rubbed his forehead like there was a pain there, but he listened through the whole song. When I finished, he didn't say anything. He certainly didn't clap for me like Ms. Maisie and her friends had.

I thought about what Ms. Maisie had said—how he had played with famous musicians. I obviously sucked at being a musician. I was never going to make it to music camp. I jerked the tube mouthpiece off the melodica and knelt down to slip it into the case.

"You closing up shop?" Saxophone Joe asked.

"Yeah. I guess I'm not too good at this."

"What was your take today?"

"Sixty-seven cents." I jammed in the melodica and zipped up the bag.

"Ouch! And a food offering." He pointed toward the splatter of hoagie bits lying in the gutter, where a couple of pigeons had descended on it.

I was sorry he saw that. I stood up and slipped the melodica case's strap over my shoulder.

"Listen here," Saxophone Joe said, "it ain't the right time of day now to be making any busking money. Kid like you, I'd say come back in the middle, late afternoon. Find yourself a piece of shade so you don't melt in the sun, sweating and swiping at your forehead, looking like you've run away from home. Literally, just run."

As soon as he said that, I couldn't help but wipe at my face.

"And you get yourself a proper box to put out for tips instead of using that flabby cloth case that looks like you left your dirty clothes out on the sidewalk." He patted his close-cropped woolly gray hair and straightened the collar of his polo shirt. "You've seen how I do. I don't go out presenting like a slob. Dress up a little."

I looked down at my saggy nylon shorts and T-shirt. They were kind of grubby.

"Might as well take advantage of your kiddie cuteness," Saxophone Joe said.

Kiddie cuteness? My face scrunched up.

He looked me up and down. "You are kinda big, but you still got that look, more kid-like than not."

I didn't appreciate that, but then I remembered all that beautiful money in his shoebox and supposed he knew what he was talking about.

"What about a permit?" I asked. "Do I need one?"

"Nah, the Altamont authorities don't require any permit as yet. But mind you be respectful of the businesspeople. Stay up close against the building so as you're not bleeding out onto the sidewalk too much, especially if you start drawing a crowd."

"Okay. Thanks. Anything else I should keep in mind?" I was beginning to think I could do this again.

"The other thing is there's an unwritten rule that you don't hog a spot for more than two hours. Gotta give someone else the chance to sing for their supper."

"Two hours. Got it." I doubted I could even last that long anyway.

"Now you know that the people out here are playing for their supper, right? This is how they make their income," Saxophone Joe said.

"Oh, sure. My dad was a musician. And I need the money too. I've got to make twenty-eight hundred dollars for my summer camp, so I can learn to be a real musician like him," I explained.

"A real musician?" Saxophone Joe raised his gray eyebrows at me.

"Like, someone who plays in a band," I said. "Gets paid for it. Writes music. Records albums."

"Seems to me playing here on the sidewalk makes for real music," Saxophone Joe said, cocking his head like I'd insulted him.

I hadn't meant to offend him. "I know. It's just that I need to get to camp so I can learn more than just show tunes." I didn't want to criticize Ms. Maisie either, but I knew music camp would open up a whole new world for me. "I just want to be able to play piano the way my dad did. Just sit down and let my fingers take over."

Saxophone Joe bobbed his head slowly, like he knew what I was talking about.

"Do you think I can really make twenty-eight hundred dollars—or at least two thousand seven hundred and eighty-two dollars and sixty-three cents—by August?" I asked, subtracting what I had from savings and the sixty-seven cents I'd made in tips.

Saxophone Joe blinked about five times before he answered. "Well, there'll be good days and bad days, but you certainly can try. It all depends on how hard you go at it. You could maybe do with a little more practice, though."

My shoulders slumped. "I practiced a ton last night. For hours. I went over every song I know."

"Just focus on a couple, maybe three songs at first and get them perfect. People don't stick around listening for any more than that," Saxophone Joe advised. "You got anything you can zone in on? Something folks might know, maybe something bluesy, and something else for the kids? You'd be amazed how much money I've made on 'You Are My Sunshine.'"

My mind raced through the repertoire of tunes I knew. "Sure, I have a couple that can work!"

"So practice on those ones, and maybe you'll make something more than loose change and leftovers."

7

That afternoon, I put on my least faded jeans and the short-sleeved, collared shirt Mom made me wear whenever Spencer was getting an award at a school ceremony. I was waiting for Pinky to come over so we could *work on our neighborhood project* when I remembered what Saxophone Joe had said about taking advantage of my kiddie cuteness. I went out to the recycling bin behind our building and dug around for a big piece of cardboard. Back inside I started to make a sign that said *SAVING FOR COLLEGE*. I thought that folks would just melt when they saw that.

Just as I was finishing up, Pinky appeared at the door I had left open. I was working on the floor on my knees and elbows, and I sat upright with a big grin so she could see my brilliant idea. She took one look at the sign and a horrified expression filled her face.

"Enly! That's not true! You're not saving for college. You can't just outright lie to people."

My grin turned upside down as I realized she was right. I threw down the marker and sat back on the floor.

"I mean the sign's a smart idea," Pinky said. "You just need a more honest message. What else can we say? How about *tips appreciated*?"

I wrinkled my nose and chewed on my lip. That was okay, but I wanted something more. "What about *saving for higher education*? Band and Jam Camp would be higher education for me, so it would technically be true."

Pinky shot her finger at the sign, signaling her approval. I flipped the cardboard over and got to work. We were heading across the overpass in no time.

Like Saxophone Joe had predicted, downtown was busier at this time of day. We had to dodge people walking along with their shopping bags and cups of iced coffee or pushing strollers full of kids. I even saw one lady with a Pekingese inside a doggie stroller.

I thought about what Saxophone Joe had said about finding shade and decided to go to the courthouse, where trees edged the plaza. The Spoon Lady was already there, clacking and stomping away, crooning out an old-time song. She had a big crowd around her and was awfully good. I imagined it would be hard to pull the crowd away from her.

Pinky and I turned back toward Altamont Books and News.

We were lucky because a banjo player was just packing up. I rushed over to take his spot and set out the Danish butter-cookie tin I had brought for tips. Behind the cookie tin, I propped up the sign.

"Look, Enly." Pinky laid out three dollar bills in the cookie tin. "Now, this is my money and you're going to give it back to me later, but I was thinking that we should put something in here to get the tips started."

"That's a great idea! Good thinking, Pinky," I said.

"Now, what're you going to play?" she asked.

I did what Saxophone Joe had suggested and practiced just a couple of songs Ms. Maisie had taught me, which I could play almost without having to completely stop to catch my breath. I brought the tube up to my mouth and started jamming on "Oh! Susanna." Pinky stood a few feet away, holding up my mom's phone to take a video for me before she began swaying her head with the music, her twisted hair swinging around her head.

People slowed down as they passed, looking my way. They were smiling, and some of them pointed at the melodica. I could tell they had never seen one. I was trying not to blare the tune too loudly, but when two ladies stopped to listen and then each threw a dollar into my tin, I got excited and couldn't help but amp up the volume.

The song ended. "Pinky, did you see that?!" I pointed at the tip box.

"Yes!" Pinky answered. "Now keep going!"

I played "Heart and Soul" next. I did pretty well with it, although it was a tad choppy because of my breath. People didn't seem to notice. Almost everyone passing looked our way, and a lot of them slowed down, mostly the people with really young kids. Parents with kids mostly seemed to drop tips, especially when they saw the sign I made. I could tell they really liked that sign.

Like Saxophone Joe had said, people didn't stay long to watch. Especially since I only had two songs. I could see that I would need to build up my repertoire with at least a couple more because sometimes the kids wanted to stay longer, but if I started to repeat a song, the parents would drag them away. That was all right with me as long as they left tips. Even coins were welcome. The sound of them clanking against the tin was music to my ears.

After a while I started to get tired. And it was kind of hot, even in the shade. Spring, even here in the mountains, could be unpredictable. Probably all that global warming.

"Pinky, I need a break. How long have I been playing?" I asked.

Pinky checked her watch. "About half an hour."

"Only half an hour!" It felt like I'd been at it all day. "Let's count the money."

"All right," Pinky agreed, "but do it quick so we don't lose too many customers."

We crouched down. Pinky removed her three dollars and slipped them into her pocket. The box looked a lot emptier.

"I'll count these," Pinky said, taking out the crumpled bills left in the box. "You count the change."

I counted the coins. "Two dollars and fifteen cents."

"Three dollars," Pinkly said.

My heart sank. "That's only five dollars and fifteen cents."

"Plus the sixty-seven cents you made this morning."

"Five dollars and eighty-two cents." I sighed.

"I don't think that's bad for only half an hour," Pinky said.

She was right. It really wasn't that bad. My mom said minimum wage was $7.25—even though the living wage, what it really cost to live in our town, was at least $17.

"If I kept making five dollars for half an hour, that would be ten dollars an hour—which is really pretty good for a kid," I said.

"Yes! I only get five a week for my allowance," Pinky said.

I did some quick computing in my head. "To make close to twenty-eight hundred dollars I would have to busk for two hundred and eighty hours." I groaned. "That seems like a lot."

"But sometimes you'll make more than this! I bet you will! Especially as you get better!"

"You really think so?" I said doubtfully.

"Yes!" Pinky fluttered the bills at me.

My mind was still calculating. "If I did two sets and worked four hours a day—and that might be a stretch to even think I could do that much—I would need to work at least seventy days to make the two hundred and eighty hours."

"Seventy days. That's only a few days more than two months," Pinky said.

"Yeah, if I worked every single day." I winced. "Which I doubt I can really do."

"Camp's not until August. That gives you plenty of time! Not even counting the times you'll make more than you've made today."

"Yeah. Maybe someone will tip me a whole sub sandwich one day," I said. "Maybe a pickle too."

"Come on, Enly!" Pinky put her hands on her hips. "You want to go to Band and Jam or not?"

I sighed. "Yes, I want to go."

"Then just play!"

8

So I kept playing.

I can't say I didn't take a lot of breaks, or that Pinky didn't have to give me a ton of pep talks when I complained that I was getting sick of my two main songs. I tried a few of the other ones I knew, but the melodica sounded too much like an angry goose.

Pinky's face soured up. "Enly, you can't play those songs until you've practiced them!" she said. "You're making too many mistakes. No one's listening. In fact, they are practically running away."

She was right. The people who passed by picked up their pace and only looked my way with their eyebrows all scrunched up when the music turned too painful for their ears. I guess it really did sound pretty awful. I went back to playing "Heart and Soul" and "Oh! Susanna" even though they were boring me out of my mind. Really, like a drill bit boring into my skull, but at least more tips came in.

At one point, after well over an hour of playing, I spotted Tia from the school bus. I stiffened as she and her friend came down the sidewalk, sipping on boba teas, but I didn't stop playing even when they stopped right in front of me. I stared right at Tia even though a wave of dread was spreading through my chest. She watched me over her straw for what seemed like forever. Then her gaze flicked down to my cookie tin. When she saw all the bills, her brows arched back, and she threw me a smirk that was different from her usual one—impressed instead of hostile. Still, Pinky and I exchanged relieved glances when she moved on.

Every five minutes or so I asked Pinky to check her phone, counting down to the end of our two-hour window. We had about twenty minutes left when I saw a little girl with two pigtails on the sides of her head come out of Mountain Discount Pharmacy with her mom just as I was finishing my song. The girl—she must have been five or six—caught sight of me right away and yanked on her mother's arm and pointed at me excitedly. Her mother was trying to stuff her long, thick wallet into her purse.

I remembered what Saxophone Joe had said about having a song for the little ones. I didn't know "You Are My Sunshine"—not yet, at least—but "There's No Business Like Show Business" sprang to mind. It was awfully catchy. I amped up my volume and began shimmying and dipping like I was playing the saxophone. Mistakes were made, but I really tried to ham it up with my moves. I was betting that wallet had a lot of money in it.

Yes! It was working. They crossed over, the little girl pretty much dragging her mom until she planted herself right in front of me. She stood there with her mouth open like I was the most amazing musician she had ever seen, though in reality it was probably just the melodica that fascinated her. Still, I played for all I was worth, ignoring my mistakes and huffing breath to finish the song with a forward toss of my head.

The little girl began jumping up and down and clapping. She had a pleated ribbon of perforated lottery tickets clutched in her hand, and it flapped like a green-and-gold banner. There must've been at least ten of them, the scratch-off kind. At my house, we called them scratchers because Spencer said that's what Dad used to call them. Apparently, Dad used to love to play the lottery. *There's always the chance*, he would say, according to Spencer. Mom said lottery tickets were a waste of money, but every Christmas she still bought a couple of them to put in our stockings as a remembrance of Dad.

"What is that thing?" the girl asked when she was done clapping.

"It's called a melodica." I held it out to her and she touched one of the keys. Of course nothing happened. "You have to blow into it at the same time." I explained. "Here, I'll blow, and then you press the key."

This time the melodica sprang to life under her hand. Her face lit up and she started doing a dance as she pecked out an awful racket. I let her keep at it until I ran out of breath. When she was done she stepped back over to her mom and yanked on her arm. "Mama, Mama!" She pointed at my cookie tin. "Tip him, tip him!"

Pinky and I grinned at each other.

The girl's mom reached into her purse and pulled out her big fat wallet. "Oh, jeez! I'm pretty sure I don't have any cash left." She glanced into it. "I'm so sorry! I spent all my cash at the pharmacy." She held up a shopping bag hooked over her arm and gave me the most sorrowful look. I tried to smile back, but the disappointment was right there, and my face felt gummy and fake.

"Mama!" the girl piped up again with a scolding note in her voice. "You always say, *If we stay, we pay.*"

"I know! I know! This is so embarrassing," her mom said as she stuffed the wallet back into her purse.

"That's okay, ma'am. I understand." I could tell she felt pretty bad, but plenty of people had stopped, watched for a minute, and just stalked off without even looking at my tip box. I'd done it plenty of times myself. But *If you stay, you pay* was a pretty good saying. Maybe I should put it on a sign.

Nah. That might turn some people off.

"Oh, and you're already saving for college." The mom put a hand to her chest. "I just love that! The cost of college has gotten ridiculous. My student loan debt is such an awful burden."

I glanced at Pinky, hoping she wouldn't say anything. I couldn't help it if the lady was making an assumption. Pinky just cocked her head at me with a scolding look.

"Oh! I know!" the mom said. "Lola, why don't you give him one of your lottery tickets?"

My eyes got big and greedy for a moment, but

when the little girl jerked the tickets to her chest with a look of panic, I said, "Oh, that's okay. I wouldn't want to give them up either. They're pretty fun." I always loved those few seconds of *vain hope*, as Mom called it, scraping away at that sticky metallic paint that hid whopping possibilities. But I never won anything anyway. I think Spencer won a dollar one year, but that was it.

I put the mouthpiece back between my lips and started playing again, scanning the street and hoping the little girl and her mom would move on since they were standing right in front of my cookie tin.

But no, they kept standing there, the girl's round eyes fixed on me as I played. After a few moments, she looked down at her chain of tickets. She started to tear the top one off, but then her hands jumped down, and ever so carefully, biting her lip in concentration, she detached three of them together. Then she dropped the three of them into my cookie tin. My eyes bugged out, but I kept playing. The girl's mom gently stroked one of her pigtails and tugged on it gently to get her to move.

As they left, Pinky yelled out, "Hey, thanks!"

I rushed through the rest of the song. Then Pinky and I dove into the cookie tin for the tickets.

"I can't believe she gave me three of them!"
I plucked them out and read the top one.

The big payday!
Top prize $5,000!
Match any of your numbers to the winning numbers, win prize shown for that number!

We squatted down. I grabbed a quarter, laid the tickets on the sidewalk, and started scraping wildly at the gold dollar sign and money sacks on the first ticket. My winning number was 7. I uncovered 1, 9, 7, 4, and 8.

"Seven and a seven! I won!" I shouted.

"You won?" Pinky screamed. "Five thousand dollars?"

I squinted at the tiny number printed under the seven. It showed $1. "No, just a dollar."

"Oh," Pinky said flatly.

I wrinkled my face, disappointed. "Weird. I won a dollar, and here I am bummed out."

"I guess when five thousand dollars is waved in front of your face, one dollar doesn't seem like much," Pinky said. "At least you got some tip money. Can I do one?"

"Sure." I tore one off for her, passed her the quarter, and watched over her shoulder while she rubbed the dollar sign.

"Winning number is four." Pinky proceeded to scrape every speck of gold off the dollar sign before she moved on to the sacks of gold.

"Then here's a two." The number showed clearly, but again, she had to scrape it clean away before moving on. It was painful to watch. "Now a nine . . . eight . . . five. And six. Darn!"

"Okay, last one." I took a big, hopeful breath and blew it out before I bent over the last ticket. "Winning number is three." This time I went slowly like Pinky had, scraping each symbol one by one and calling out the numbers as they appeared.

"Nine."

"Four."

"Seven."

"One."

"Three."

"Three!" I shouted. My heart started racing.

"How much? How much?!" Pinky demanded.

I already had the card right up to my face, my eyelids peeled back in disbelief, my jaw fallen practically to the ground. "*Three thousand!* Is that right?"

I rubbed my eyes to make sure I didn't have gunk in them that was making me see things wrong. "Does it really say three thousand?"

"Enly, you'd better not be kidding me," Pinky warned. "Let me see that!"

I turned the card toward her. She squinted and raised her pointed finger at the tiny print. "Three thousand." She moved her finger down a tad. "And three thousand!" Her eyes got really big. "Yep, that's what it says. Enly, you won three thousand dollars!"

We both got up and started jumping and flapping out our excitement. People went by, looking at us like we'd lost our minds.

"That's your Band and Jam money! You're going to Band and Jam! We're both going to Band and Jam!" Pinky hollered.

I peered at the card again. The numbers danced before my eyes. "I can't believe it!" We started gathering everything up. "Let's go cash it in right now!"

9

We ran across the street to Mountain Discount Pharmacy. The store was pretty small, not like a chain drugstore. There was a single long rack down the center, and it was low enough that you could see the whole store in one glance. Several customers were scattered around, mostly at the back where the prescriptions were filled or at the tall beverage coolers along the wall near the front checkout. A few people were waiting in line at the register. We got behind them and bounced on our toes, still bursting with excitement.

"I can't believe it!" I said. "I just can't believe it!" I checked the card again to make sure that the winning number and my number were both really threes, that *$3,000* was really printed under my number three. Yep, it all checked out. In a few months

I would be onstage with Pinky, pounding out the tunes on a full-size keyboard. Maybe there would even be a baby grand piano there. Heck, maybe I'd do a few sets with my melodica. My good old melodica. I patted it where it hung on my shoulder in its carrying bag.

"Your mom is going to be so surprised!" Pinky squealed.

My stomach flipped. Mom.

"She's going to be so happy!" Pinky said.

Hmm. My stomach tightened. Of course she was going to be happy that I'd won three thousand dollars, but she would probably insist that I give the money to Spencer for college.

The line moved forward. Pinky chattered away, but I wasn't listening. As long as I could remember, Mom had had a plan and only one plan. Spencer would go to college no matter how hard she—and he—had to work. He would get a degree, find a good-paying job, and then turn around and help me through college. There was never any discussion of whether or not I *wanted* to go to college. In all honesty, I didn't even really think about it much. That was so far away for me. I just wanted to play my music now.

If I went to Band and Jam, maybe I would be a real musician by the time I graduated from high school, and I wouldn't even need to go to college. But Mom probably wouldn't accept that kind of argument, not after what had happened to Dad. She must've known that Dad was all into music when she married him, but since he died and left her on her own with us, it seemed like she thought more like Grandma—concentrating on what was safe and secure.

But this ticket was my shot at going to music camp. I couldn't just give it up. I wouldn't. Instead of taking the chance of Mom giving the money to Spencer, I would somehow have to send the money straight to Band and Jam once I had the cash.

"Next, please!" The clerk called us to the counter, and Pinky and I stepped up.

I slapped the lottery ticket on the counter and pushed it toward her. "Three thousand dollars, please."

The clerk ducked her head forward and looked at me through her bangs. Her long fingernails were painted bright pink, and they clicked against the counter as she picked up the ticket. A pair of glasses hung from a chain around her neck. She put them on and took her time studying the card. "Well, looky here. I do believe you've got a winning card!" She set the ticket on the counter and slid it back toward me. "Now you better run this back to your parents. You're supposed to be eighteen to play." She winked at me. "Or at least to claim any prize money. But you know, we don't cash that much here. Your mama or daddy has to take it down to the regional office in Raleigh."

"The regional office in Raleigh?" I repeated blankly.

"Yes, baby. Local establishments don't cash anything over six hundred dollars. Those big winnings have to be awarded at regional. Next, please!"

She was already looking over our heads, so I took the ticket, and Pinky and I shuffled out of the way of a couple of teenagers behind us. Pinky started toward the door, but I stopped her. "Wait a minute," I said.

"What is it?" Pinky asked.

I didn't answer her at first, just stared at all the candy on the rack next to the counter.

"Are you going to buy something?" Pinky rattled the cookie tin she was carrying for me. "I guess it won't hurt to spend some of this now that you have the three thousand dollars."

"That's the problem, Pinky. If I ask my mom to cash the scratcher for me, she'll say we have to use the money for Spencer's college."

"Really? That's not fair! It's your money! You need that money to pay for camp!"

"I know, but she thinks college is more important." It wasn't that I didn't want to help Spencer—I just wanted to do this one thing. This one big thing. It was big for me anyway, though Mom would probably never understand. Maybe it wasn't as important as going to college, but Spencer was so smart and good at studying that I was really, really sure he would rake in plenty of scholarship money.

One of the guys who had been in line behind us interrupted. "Hey, you're Spencer's little brother, aren't you?" He had a messy thatch of blond hair and brown freckles all over his pale face.

I nodded.

"I'm Archie. And this is Randy." Archie gestured toward the other guy, who was a head shorter than him, closer to my height and sort of bulky like me, but much more muscly. He was pretty tanned for it to be only spring.

"Yeah," said Randy, "Spencer's a friend of ours. So you had a big win? That's great. Congratulations!"

"Thanks," I said.

"We couldn't help but overhear you guys talking," Archie said. "Your problem with your lottery ticket."

"Yeah, man," Randy said. "That bites. You shouldn't have to hold off on your dream of going to camp."

"It really isn't fair!" Pinky said.

"You know, that's pretty selfish of Spencer," Archie said. "I can't imagine him going along with something like that. I bet he'd be happy for you to go to camp."

"Yeah, probably," I agreed. Spencer wasn't mean or selfish, really. Except about free ice cream.

"Listen, I just turned eighteen." Archie scraped a hand through his hair. "If you want, I'll cash the ticket for you."

"Really?" My eyebrows shot up. I glanced at Pinky. Her eyebrows were up too. For a second I thought my problem was solved, but then I remembered what the clerk had said about where we had to go to get paid out. "The office is over in Raleigh. Isn't that like three hours away? My mom wouldn't just let me go to Raleigh with a couple of eighteen-year-olds, even if you're friends of Spencer's. She'd want to know why."

Archie turned out his hands. "I guess you wouldn't have to come. We could cash it for you and bring the money back."

I looked at Pinky, not sure. Her head bounced just the tiniest bit as if she thought that it was a pretty good plan. But I hated to let the card out of my sight.

"How do you know Spencer again?" I'd never heard Spencer mention anyone named Archie or Randy.

"We're in Math Club together," Archie said.

Randy elbowed Archie and added, "Yeah, we *were*. Last year, before we graduated, that is."

"Oh," I said. "Well, um . . ." I looked at the lottery ticket between my fingers. "Maybe let me talk to . . ."

"Yeah, that's a good idea. Ask Spencer about us." Archie reached over and plucked the ticket out of my hand. "I'll get the money from the regional office and meet you here tomorrow, same time, okay?" Then he and Randy bolted out the door.

10

Pinky and I looked at each other. My chest felt tight, and she was biting her lips like she wasn't sure what had just happened.

"I have a bad feeling about this," she said.

We hurried outside and looked down the sidewalk, which was crowded with people walking in and out of the shops and restaurants. I craned my neck in both directions but didn't see any sign of Archie or Randy.

"Well, they definitely know Spencer," I said nervously, trying to convince myself that everything was fine.

"Do they?" Pinky grabbed my arm. "Or did they just overhear you talking about him?"

My stomach soured.

"Wait!" Pinky said. "They said they used to be in

Math Club together. We didn't say anything about Math Club! Is Spencer in Math Club?"

My heart bobbed with hope. "Yes. Yes, he sure is! He started the club himself!"

"So there you go!" Pinky threw her hand up in the air. "Phew! I was worried for a minute."

I didn't say anything. We started walking down the sidewalk. I didn't know where we were going. I just let Pinky lead the way because the burbling in my gut was talking to me.

Then I realized why.

"Pinky!" I halted in my tracks. "Spencer just started Math Club this year. There wasn't any club last year. It was my mom's idea for him to start it up, something else to help him score scholarships for college."

Pinky frowned. "So, what does that mean?"

"Those guys couldn't have been in Math Club last year. They were lying!" I wanted to cry.

Pinky's eyes got big. "You mean those guys just stole your ticket!"

11

I tried to swallow, but my mouth was dry. My tongue felt like a piece of cardboard.

"Oh, jeez!" Pinky clutched her head with one hand, still gripping my tip box with her other one. "That was your ticket to Band and Jam! That was three thousand dollars! *Three thousand dollars!*"

She didn't have to tell me. I couldn't believe I had handed over $3,000 just like that to a couple of scam artists.

"We have to get that ticket back!" I started marching in the direction of the police station on Patton Avenue. "We need to report a theft!"

Pinky hustled after me, trying to keep up. "Hold on, Enly. Are you sure it's a good idea to get the police involved?"

Honestly, I *wasn't* sure. They would want to drag

our parents into the situation. I could just imagine Mom getting a call from the police while she was at work. She would freak out, and even when she found out I wasn't really in trouble, she would see it as trouble—having to talk to police officers during work hours, maybe even having to come down to the station. And if I got the ticket back, I was sure she would lock up the money in the bank.

We hadn't gone more than a block before I spotted a patrol officer on a bike.

"Officer! Officer!" I threw up an arm and waved, trying to get the officer to stop.

The patrol officer veered next to us between two cars. A braid of red hair hung down from beneath her helmet. Her uniform was shorts and a black-and-yellow shirt with a badge and a name tag that said *Officer K. Petty.* "Hey, kids, what's up?"

Now that a police officer was actually standing in front of us, I froze up and Pinky sprang into action. "Officer, we've been robbed!" Pinky said.

"Robbed?" Officer Petty frowned as she dismounted and pulled the bike up onto the sidewalk.

"Yes!" Pinky elbowed me. "Tell her, Enly."

"I had this lottery ticket, you see, and we found out that we weren't old enough to cash it. These two guys offered to help us get it cashed, and they took it and ran off." The words came out in an embarrassed tumble.

"Ooookayyyy," Officer Petty drawled like she was trying to understand.

"It was worth three thousand dollars!" Pinky jumped in.

"Whoa! That's a lot of money. Now, back up a minute. How did you get the ticket, and why didn't your parents cash it?" She placed one hand on her hip while still holding the bike with the other.

"I was busking"—I twisted around to show her the melodica case on my shoulder—"and someone tipped me with some scratchers. Scratch-off lottery tickets, I mean . . ." I explained about going to the pharmacy to cash the winning ticket and finding out we weren't old enough.

"The guys who were standing behind us in the pharmacy offered to do it," Pinky added. "They said they knew Enly's brother. He's sixteen."

"So you gave them the ticket?" Officer Petty grimaced. "That doesn't sound quite like a robbery."

Pinky and I looked at each other, totally deflated. I swallowed. "But they snatched it out of my hand before I really agreed to it."

"Yeah," Pinky said, "they tricked us! What's that word . . . ?" She snapped her fingers trying to come up with it.

"Fraud!" I shouted. "That's right. They frauded us!"

Officer Petty dipped her head like she understood. "Did you sign that ticket?" Officer Petty asked.

I shook my head.

"I suppose if you had signed it, that would've nullified the ticket and at least prevented anyone else from getting the money. But your brother knows these guys, right?"

"They said they used to go to school with him, but we're pretty sure they lied."

"Hmm." Officer Petty put both her hands on the handlebars of her bike, bounced the front wheel, and glanced down both directions of the street. I hoped she was thinking about which way to start chasing them. "Did you get their names?" she asked.

"Yes! Archie and Randy," I said.

"Last names?"

Pinky and I both shook our heads.

"But if they went to Altamont High, they'll be in the yearbook!" I pictured the row of yearbooks lined up on the bookshelf next to Spencer's bed. Spencer was thrifty like Mom, but he did spring for the year-book every year.

"That's true!" Officer Petty nodded. "Good thinking. But what makes you think that these guys aren't going to do what they said—cash the ticket and hand the money back to you?"

"We just know," I said glumly, thinking again about the Math Club lie. "I need to get it back. Please say you can help us!"

Officer Petty sighed. "Kids, I'm afraid you're right that you've been tricked, but with you both being underage, I'm not sure you have any legal recourse in claiming that ticket, even if those guys are found." She gave us a pained smile. "Your parents should go down to the station and file a report if they want to pursue it as a theft or fraud. They can ask for me, Officer Petty, but even then if the case gets picked up and the guys are found, it's going to be your word against theirs."

Pinky and I looked at each other again. I felt like my insides had all spilled out. "It's Saturday, so I'm sure the claims office won't be open until Monday," Officer Petty added. "The way I see it, you ought to check with your brother and see if he knows the guys. If he does, then maybe your parents can have a talk with them or their parents."

"Can you at least keep an eye out for them?" Pinky asked.

She offered up a sympathetic smile. "Sure. Tell me what they looked like. If I see them on my rounds, I could have a little word with them."

Pinky gave Officer Petty a really good description of the guys, mentioning things like freckles, braided string bracelets, and blue sneakers.

After Office Petty rode off, Pinky turned to me. "What now? You want me to go with you to tell your mom?"

I chewed the inside of my cheek, thinking. "Nah, I'm pretty certain Mom won't want to get involved with this. She doesn't have the time, and she won't want to run around town having arguments or trying to reason with people she doesn't know." Besides that, I still didn't want her to know about the ticket if there was any possible way I could get it back myself.

"Oh. You want to tell my mom or dad? They might help."

"No! They'll tell my mom about it, and then if we did get the ticket back, I'll be right back at the beginning with no money for camp, because I know what my mom will do with it. I have to find a way to get it back on my own."

Pinky smacked her tongue against the roof of her mouth in frustration. "Enly, what can you do? I think it's best to tell at least one of our parents and let them figure out how to help."

"I said no, Pinky!"

Pinky reared her head back at my sharp tone. Her eyebrows were raised high on her forehead.

"Sorry, sorry," I mumbled. "Can you help me think of something else?"

Pinky sighed. "I don't know, Enly. Maybe we should give up on the ticket. It's lost and even if we got it back, who would cash it for you if not your mom?"

"We'll figure that out later!"

Pinky sighed again, more heavily this time. "This is getting to be too much. Just forget about it."

"But it's my camp money!"

"So you get the money some other way." Pinky held up the cookie tin. "Go back to busking."

"That's two hundred and eighty hours of work!" At least.

"Well, if that's what it takes . . ." Her shoulder hiked up and she flipped her free hand palm-up.

Something about that gesture pushed me over the edge. "Yeah, easy for you to say!"

"What's that supposed to mean?"

"Piano lessons, dance lessons, vacations, music camp. It's all so easy for you. Everything you want is just handed to you."

Pinky's nostril flared. "Don't try to make me feel bad because my parents can afford nice things. They work hard for their money."

"And my mom doesn't? My mom works harder than anyone!"

"Enly! I didn't say anything about your mom! All I'm saying is, don't blame this on me. I've been trying to help you, remember?"

"Wow, how generous of you—helping out a charity case like me!"

"That's not what I . . ."

"Why'd you even bother showing me the camp brochure? You weren't really thinking about *me* at all. You just wanted a sidekick at camp. But the reality is that you still get to go whether I can or not. If *you* had to work for the tuition, you wouldn't act like it's no big deal. You wouldn't be judging me and bossing me around if you knew what this was really like."

She stared at me, shaking her head as if to say, *What the . . .*

I just glared back at her. I knew she was waiting for me to apologize, but all I could do was listen to the blood rushing around in my ears.

Pinky finally closed her mouth and blinked several times. "You know what? I'm going home. I came out here to support you, but you think you know everything. So do it your way and good luck with that!" She spun around.

I watched as she marched down the sidewalk with my cookie tin still tucked up under one arm.

I had an awful churning in my stomach, not sure what had just happened. I knew better than to make comparisons. It wasn't that I resented her for having everything she wanted without lifting a finger . . .

Well, maybe I did just a tiny bit.

She had no idea what it was like to want something so much and have it almost in reach, only to have it taken away again. She just didn't understand.

But I knew someone who might.

12

Supreme Cream was just on the next corner. Luckily it was close to dinnertime, so there weren't any customers inside. The door chimed as I entered. Spencer was sitting on a stool by the cash register, his head bent over his AP calculus textbook with his glasses off. His boss, knowing that Spencer was such a serious student, didn't mind if he studied when business was slow. When it came to Spencer, people always *admired his determination* and wanted to help *foster his talent*.

"What are you doing here?" Spencer said when he put his glasses back on and saw me. "No, you can't have any free samples." Free samples were always allowed to everyone except for me. When Spencer first started working, I came in demanding to try all the flavors. Spencer put a stop to that by telling Mom that I was distracting him at work.

"I don't want ice cream. Listen, so I had this lottery ticket and two guys who said they knew you stole it from me. It was worth—"

"Wait a minute, wait a minute," Spencer said. "Start over. How'd you get a lottery ticket? I thought you had to be eighteen to buy them."

I launched into the whole story, starting with the busking, though I didn't mention my fight with Pinky. Spencer blinked double-time when I said *three thousand dollars*. His mouth dropped open at the part about the two guys. Then frown lines crinkled on his forehead when I said they'd claimed to know him.

"What were their names?" Spencer asked.

"Archie and Randy," I told him. "We didn't get their last names."

Spencer groaned and shook his head.

"I know, I know. I shouldn't have let them take it," I said. "But it was because I thought they knew you. They talked about Math Club."

"Oh, I know who they are."

I took a big breath and exhaled, absolutely relieved. "You do?"

"Archie Sanger and Randy O'Neil." He rose from his stool and slammed his calculus book shut.

"Total jerks! They both live in the neighborhood. But they've sure never been in Math Club. They ride my bus, and I have Personal Finance class with them."

"You mean they're still in school? They told us that they graduated last year. That they were old enough to cash out the ticket." I was starting to feel mixed-up again.

"I doubt they're eighteen," Spencer said. "Unless they failed a year or two, which I don't think they have. They're in my grade."

"So that means they can't cash the ticket either!"

"Maybe not, but their parents sure could. Why didn't you give it to Mom?" Spencer asked me.

I sighed. "Because she'd take the money for college. Your college. But I wanted to use it for music camp this summer."

"Oh brother!" Spencer groaned again.

"I have plans too, you know! We can't all be super brains."

"You're as smart as I am. Just lazy." He was repeating what Mom always said about me.

"I'm not lazy! I just don't want to think about college yet. I'm only in middle school. But what about the scratcher? You've got to help me get it back!"

Spencer shook his head. "They've probably already given it to one of their parents to cash."

A groan wheezed out of me, all my hope whiffling away. Then I remembered that it was Saturday.

"But they couldn't have cashed it yet! They have to go to the claims office in Raleigh and it's probably not open today!" I was practically shouting.

"Yeah, probably not," Spencer agreed.

"Do you know where they live? You have to go to their house! You can talk to them. Or even better, tell their parents that the ticket belongs to us and that they stole it. They'll listen to you!"

Spencer made a face, but I was sure they *would* listen to him. Not only did Spencer have the nerdy study habits and perfect grades that always had teachers and parents drooling over him, but he was also polite and thoughtful, like he was already an adult. It was so annoying.

"You have to help me, Spencer. Please!"

Spencer's forehead crumpled up. I knew he didn't want to do it because really, he wasn't the type of person who wanted to get into any kind of conflict. He was skinny and wore thick glasses, and even though he was sixteen, he was only slightly taller than me. Of course, I was big for my age. His hand-me-downs never fit me, and Mom had to buy husky jeans for me. We couldn't have been more different.

"Please, Spencer. I never ask you to do anything for me. If you help with this, I'll wash all the dishes and take out the trash and clean the bathroom for the rest of the year," I promised desperately.

He shook his head.

"Please!" I begged. "You're my only hope!"

He rolled his eyes at me, but then he glanced at the clock. "I have twenty minutes until the end of my shift. Wait for me outside."

"Yes! Yes. Thank you, thank you!"

13

Spencer ranted at me under his breath as we left Supreme Cream and headed back into our neighborhood. "How could you let this happen? It's ridiculous! To be bamboozled like that. Absolutely bamboozled." Spencer always used words that made him sound like he should live at the Olmstead Apartments with the old folks. I didn't think he really expected an answer to his question, because he kept grumbling. "You'd think you'd know better with three thousand dollars! You don't deserve to have that kind of money if you just let it fall out of your hands like that."

I kept quiet. I didn't care what he said about me. I was just glad he was going to help me get my ticket back. I knew he was nervous, probably even a bit scared, because of the way he swung his head and kept saying, "I can't believe I'm doing this! It's not going to work. Those guys are not going to hand it over just like that! And why would their parents believe me over their own kid?"

We stopped on the sidewalk outside a brick ranch house with a fenced-in yard. Leafy hydrangea bushes grew all around the front and sides of the house. "I think this is Randy's place," Spencer said.

I'd noticed the house before, for two reasons. One was that I'd seen a pig in the yard. Not a cute little pink one, but a ginormous, brown-black bristly girl the size of a small bear. In fact, the first time I saw her, I'd thought it *was* a bear, since they ambled into town sometimes to dig around in people's trash. Some people had a few chickens, but this was the only pig I'd ever seen around. I knew the pig was female because she has a bunch of . . . pig udders, I guess you'd call them, hanging from her underside.

Randy's house was also the only one in the neighborhood with a pool, one of those big above-ground ones. Part of it was visible from the sidewalk because the yard around the house was so wide. As we stood there, I heard a loud slap of water and splashing, as if someone had just jumped into the pool.

"They must be back there!" I said. "What are you going to do?"

Spencer scowled at me.

"I mean *we*," I corrected myself. "What should we do?"

He glanced around. "The carport is empty. I guess his parents aren't home." He didn't say anything else, just stood there twitching his mouth like he was thinking.

I waited, glancing around for the pig. I didn't see her anywhere. I figured there must be a pen for her in the back. Finally, I prodded Spencer. "Should we go around back?"

He hesitated. "Let's just take a look first."

He swung the gate open and we crossed the front yard, moving toward the side of the house. Spencer kept herding me closer and closer to the house until we were nearly in the bushes. We peered into the back. The pool was in the center of the yard. Under a tree, there was a wooden structure in a small, straw-covered section of the yard surrounded by a wire fence. The gate to the fence was open, but the dark mound of the pig was lying halfway under the structure.

Archie was lying on an inflatable pool lounger with his blond hair and pale feet visible to us. The back of Randy's dark head bobbed beside him, his arm hooked over a pool noodle.

"It's them!" I whispered fiercely.

Spencer elbowed me hard and whipped his finger up to his lips to shush me. We crouched down.

"I can't believe I got that ticket away from him so easily," Archie snorted.

They were talking about me! My face burned.

"How long do you think it's going to take for him to figure out that we're not going to bring him the money?" Randy said. "Think he'll run home and tell his big brother all about it? You shouldn't have told him our names."

"I wasn't thinking. Who cares anyway? His big brother's a wimp—all I'd have to do is say boo to that skinny beanpole and he'd run away." Archie hooted, then rolled off the lounger and sank underwater.

Spencer's mouth pinched up, and his eyes narrowed. He pushed his glasses farther up the bridge of his nose. I could tell he was mad, and he hardly ever got mad.

"Look!" I said between my teeth and pointed around the corner of the house. Spencer craned his neck to see, then pulled his head back and gave me a look that said, *So what?*

"The sliding glass doors," I muttered, working hard to stay quiet even though a wave was building inside me. "They're wide open!"

Spencer gave me impatient bug eyes, another *So what?* look.

"They're in their swimsuits, so they can't have the lottery ticket on them," I explained. "It must be inside somewhere!"

"And? What do you expect me to do, run inside and look around?" He scowled.

I realized it was a bad idea. If Spencer got caught creeping into someone's house, he might get arrested. It would go on his record. His chances of getting into college could be ruined. And Mom would be furious.

But the ticket had to be inside! It was probably sitting there tucked in the pocket of Archie's pants. I was absolutely certain of it.

14

Before I knew what I was doing, I'd slipped my melodica case from my shoulder, set it on the ground, and edged around the corner of the house.

Spencer grabbed my pant leg. "What are you doing?!" he hissed.

I kicked his hand off and kept crawling, moving toward the sliding glass doors, keeping low so the guys wouldn't see me over the high rim of the pool.

A half-circle-shaped flagstone patio with a bunch of deck chairs scattered on it led to the doors. I wormed behind the chairs, hoping they would give me cover. Water splashed and the guys were still talking, but I couldn't make out what they were saying because blood roared in my ears. I didn't dare glance at the pool or back at Spencer. My eyes were trained on the doorway just a few yards away.

Then just a few feet away. Then I was commando-crawling across the threshold onto the beige carpet of the living room.

My heart was banging in my chest as I scrambled to the side of the door, out of the boys' line of sight. I didn't realize I had been holding my breath until it came out in a low, shaky huff.

I paused to calm myself down and take everything in. The kitchen and dining room were on one side of the wide living room, which was neat and tidy with the furniture clustered in the center of the room. A big picture window looked out onto the front yard. On the right were the bedrooms. With one glance at an unmade bed, posters on the wall, and clothes on the floor, I knew the one closest to me had to be Randy's room.

My heart was still thumping, but I stood up and darted into the bedroom. The room smelled sort of skunky, and my face went *blech* as I dropped down to sift through the clothes that were scattered all over the place. I couldn't remember what the guys had been wearing, so I picked up each pair of pants and shorts and checked every pocket. Disgusting underwear was still stuck inside a bunch of them, making me dry-heave a few times.

But there was no ticket.

I tried the shirts. Some of them had pockets at the chest. I even poked at the socks.

But no ticket.

Where could it be? Frantically, I rose to scan the top of the dresser. It was loaded with all kinds of junk—deodorant, barbells, pens, body sprays, books, loose change, keys, a wallet.

When I saw the wallet, I suddenly had the most terrible rush of excitement and anxiety all mixed up. The scratcher had to be there. I just knew it.

But here I was. I hadn't quite broken into someone's house, but I had sneaked in. Was I going to paw through someone's wallet and possibly take something from it? That felt like crossing a line. But at the same time, my brain screamed that the ticket was mine. I had a right to it!

The voices in the backyard were getting louder. The bedroom window faced the backyard. It was closed, but the voices sounded angry and I could tell that someone was getting out of the water. My eyes jumped around for a place to hide. The bed!

I dove under it, struggling to wedge myself in, my face scraping roughly on the carpet. It was a tight fit, and I had to shove aside smelly balled-up socks, scrunched-up wrappings from fast food, old shoes, and dusty toys that probably hadn't seen the light of day in years. I shrank as far under as I possibly could, pinching my nose against the dust and ignoring the pain of something hard poking me in the hip.

Someone stomped in. I couldn't tell for sure if it was Archie or Randy, but judging by the pale feet, I guessed it was Archie. Water dripped onto the carpet as he slapped the towel to dry himself. He pushed his swim trunks off and left them in a wet pile on the floor before he started putting on his pants, muttering under his breath the whole time. The only thing I made out was, "He's out of his mind! No way I'm giving . . . !"

My armpits were clammy with sweat. Afraid I would sneeze if I let go of my nose, I could only breathe out of my mouth.

Archie huffed around the room, collecting a sleeping bag, pad, and duffle bag, which had been crammed into the corner. Now I was sure it was him, gathering up his spending-the-night gear.

He stopped in the middle of the room. All his stuff dropped to the floor. The feet moved toward the bed. I went rigid.

The bed sagged as Archie plopped down on it. He picked up one of his sneakers and lifted one foot.

I didn't even have a moment to be relieved before I noticed his other shoe next to my head. It was just a matter of time before he ducked down to look for it. Frantically, I pushed it closer to his foot, the tip of it peeking out from under the bed. I prayed that he didn't see it move.

Archie grabbed the shoe and jammed his foot into it.

I was scared to breathe. I stared across the room, willing him to hurry up.

That's when I caught sight of my scratcher tucked into the frame of the mirror attached to the dresser. The glossy green and gold seemed to wink at me. I had to bite down hard on my lips to not yelp with excitement.

Archie stood up, grabbed his stuff, and left the bedroom.

My mouth flew open and again I had to muffle a gasp. He had left the ticket behind! My heart started to hammer wildly in my chest. He had forgotten it. I couldn't believe my luck. I was going to get my scratcher back!

But in the next second, Archie returned, snorting out a laugh. He plucked the ticket out of the mirror's frame just like he had snatched it out of my fingertips.

The blood drained from my face as he kissed the ticket, slipped it into the pocket of his T-shirt, and left.

15

Although I felt like crying as Archie disappeared with my scratcher, I knew I had to get out of the house. What was going on outside? Had Randy stayed in the pool? Spencer was probably freaking out. Was it safe for me to wiggle out from under the bed?

I strained to hear anything from the window over the bed, but instead I heard a strange, soft snuffling noise coming from the living room. It got louder, closer, moving toward the bedroom. The next thing I knew, Randy's huge black pig was at the bedroom door.

I caught myself before a yelp escaped me. Frozen in fear, I watched as she ambled in, sniffing at all the dirty socks and underwear, poking at them with her snout.

When she came to the bed and pushed her snout under it, near my face, I tried to wedge myself farther back, but there was nowhere to go. Her face was all smooshed up with rolls of thick skin that even hung down over her eyes. As she prodded her snout at me, snorting and getting excited, I had a sudden fear that she was going to bite me. I wasn't sure if pigs attacked and bit people like a dog might, but I thought I'd read that they eat just about anything.

"Go away! Shoo, shoo," I hissed. I tried to flap her away but I was scared my fingers would be chomped. I patted around me for some of those crumpled food wrappers. When I found one I tossed it away from the bed as best I could.

She twisted away to whiff at it. Her body and pig udders—teats, I think they're really called—were right at my eye level. For some reason, it embarrassed me to look at them.

"Biscuit!" Randy bellowed from just outside the bedroom door. "What are you doing in here?"

There was a flash of feet. Randy crossed over to Biscuit, who was still rooting at the fast-food trash.

"Come on, girl." He tried to get her to leave, but Biscuit wasn't budging. "Come on! You're not supposed to be inside." The harder he pushed her, the more she backed up toward the bed. Finally, she plopped down. I suppressed a groan. Her behind was right next to my face and she reeked of pig—not as bad as you'd think a pig smelled, but nothing like bacon.

"Fine!" Randy gave up. "You're going to have to deal with Mom," he said to Biscuit.

The mattress creaked over me. Oh, jeez! Randy had stretched out on it. If he took a nap or something, I was going to be stuck here all evening. Between him above me and Biscuit beside me, I was beginning to feel like I was running out of air.

"Hey," he said, "what're you doing?"

After a second I realized he must be talking to someone on his phone. His voice wasn't angry, so I didn't think Archie was on the other end.

"Just got out of the pool," he said.

Pause.

"He left," Randy said. "Had a hissy fit, took his stuff and the ticket."

My ears pricked up. He was talking about Archie.

Randy continued with scorn in his voice. "What a jerk! He wants to keep it all for himself to go toward the car he wants to buy."

There was a long pause while whoever was on the other end talked. Biscuit, done with the wrapper, began to push her snout under the bed again, down near my ankles. I couldn't move around much but I wiggled the best I could, trying to find something else for her so she wouldn't eat my leg while I struggled to hear what Randy was saying over Biscuit's snuffling.

"Yeah, he'll come around," Randy said on the phone. "His parents aren't going to be back until the middle of next week. He's supposed to stay with us while they're away, and if he doesn't show up for dinner, my parents will have questions. I told him that I'll tell them about that ticket—that he stole it— if he doesn't share it with . . ."

Randy broke off because the doorbell started ringing, and someone was pounding on the front door.

"What the . . . I'll call you back. Someone's at the door. I bet it's him!"

This was my chance. I had to get Biscuit to move as soon as Randy left the room. I started twitching around even before Randy was off the bed. Biscuit ignored me, but whatever had been sticking under my hip shifted. I put my hand on it, and right away I knew that it was one of those small toy dart guns that clack when you shoot them, even if they're not loaded.

I felt Randy lift off the mattress. The doorbell was still ringing over and over. I counted to five, the number of steps I thought it'd take to leave the room, then pulled the trigger on the dart gun. A foam dart shot out and popped Biscuit in the butt. She jumped up as much as a giant animal with short legs could and moved away from the bed.

I scrambled out and jetted across the bedroom, slowing just for a second at the doorframe. Randy's bare back was at the front door, towel wrapped around his hips. I bolted to the sliding glass doors, not even bothering to duck behind the couch.

As I ran out and across the patio, I felt the hair on the back of my neck prick up, expecting Randy to shout out at me, chase me. I sped toward the side of the house. Already I was looking to break for the gate, the street, but as I turned the corner of the house, someone grabbed me. An arm hooked me around the waist and a hand clamped over my mouth as I was pulled into the bushes.

I started to thrash around, throwing out my arms and kicking, but there was fierce shushing in my ear. It was Spencer. He let go of my mouth and loosened his grip on my body, but he kept his arms around me. The expression on his face told me to sit still.

"Archie, I know it's you!" Randy shouted angrily from the front of the house.

He was silent for a moment. We were silent.

"You're being a jerk!" he howled. The front door slammed.

I looked at Spencer.

He nodded.

We ran.

16

We flew past house after house in the neighborhood and only slowed down after we turned a couple of corners. Spencer was still striding fast while I clumped behind him, trying to keep up. I was grateful to see he had my melodica slung across his back. After another block of speed-walking, he stopped on the sidewalk and spun around. "Are you out of your mind?"

I opened my mouth to defend myself, but he cut me off.

"That was basically breaking and entering. What the heck were you thinking?"

"I guess . . . well." I shrugged, but Spencer thrust his head forward, still waiting for me to answer. "I guess I thought if *you* went in there and got caught, it would've messed everything up for you," I stammered. "You would get in big trouble, but I'm just a kid—I mean you are too, but I'm closer to a kid-kid. And since it was my scratcher—I thought I should do the dirty work." I knew this didn't sound convincing. The truth was, I hadn't really thought it through.

Spencer practically growled, "For one thing, *I* would never have considered breaking into someone's house."

"I didn't break in," I protested weakly. "The door was open." A wave of heat crept up to my ears as the wallet I had almost searched came to mind. I was glad my face was already flushed from running so that Spencer wouldn't notice my embarrassment.

Spencer gave me a look, but then he dropped the subject. "Did you get the ticket back?"

"No," I admitted. "But I got out okay!"

"Yeah, thanks to me getting Randy to the door."

"Ooooh, that was you! That was so smart, dude!" I gave him a big grin. "Really, really smart!" I laid it on thick, hoping to improve his mood.

It didn't work. He shot me one last annoyed look, thrust my melodica at me, and started walking fast again.

I loped after him, worrying that he was going to give up on the ticket. "Archie has the ticket, Spencer.

I saw him put it in his shirt pocket. He and Randy had a fight, and Archie—"

"I know. I heard the whole thing while I was hiding in the bushes, waiting for you to get pummeled or arrested and sent to juvie," Spencer said.

"So what are we going to do now?" I asked.

"We're going home."

I stopped on the sidewalk. "Home? Why?"

Spencer didn't even slow down. He just shook his head.

"No. Wait!" I shouted. "Please, Spencer!"

"After what you pulled!" he yelled over his shoulder. "You're right about one thing—we're going to get in trouble with your ideas."

I hurried to catch up with him. "No, I won't do anything like that again! Let's just go talk to Archie like our original plan. You can convince him to give it back. Randy is already mad and threatening to tell Archie's parents that he took the ticket from me. We can tell him that Randy has already told them, or . . . I don't know, something."

Spencer flicked his hand and shook his head.

I grabbed his arm and pulled him to a stop. "Spencer, it's three thousand dollars! They took it from me." I had a tight, heaving feeling in my chest.

"It's *my* money! It's the only way I'll ever get to do anything like Band and Jam."

"It probably still wouldn't be enough." He yanked his arm out of my grasp. "Taxes, Enly. Have you thought about how the prize will probably be taxed?"

I hadn't, but it couldn't be all that much. "I can make up the rest by busking. I'm a musician. Like Dad! Dad wouldn't give up!"

"Yeah, and look what happened to him," Spencer said flatly.

I was speechless for a moment, horrified that Spencer was invoking Grandma's and Mom's notion that music was to blame for Dad's death.

"Spencer!" I shook my head in disbelief. How could he so easily brush aside Dad's and my aspirations? Squash them, really. How could he be so pessimistic? "Don't say that!" Tears were threatening to push out. I blinked hard, trying to hold them in, because I hated crying in front of him. "Dad was determined. Hopeful!"

Spencer's eyes shifted to the sidewalk. I could tell he was sorry, that he wanted to take back what he'd said.

"Come on, let's at least try!" I pressed. "Remember what you told me Dad always said: *There's always the chance.* He said it about lottery tickets, and that ticket I got from busking was finally our big win. We can't just give up and forget about it!"

An odd feeling came over me as I suddenly realized the coincidence—winning lottery ticket, Dad, music camp. Spencer seemed to register the weirdness of it as well because he suddenly looked completely thrown off.

I swiped at the sweat on my face and took a few deep breaths. "Please. It means everything to me."

Spencer sighed heavily. He was caving! "Come on," he said as he started walking.

My heart leaped as I followed him, although I wasn't absolutely sure of what he'd decided. Was he going to help me, or was he heading home? My tongue itched to ask, but I thought better of pestering him, especially if he was trying to come up with a plan.

17

Spencer halted when we came to a blue two-story house with a pointy roof and a wide front porch. Archie was sitting in a chair with his feet propped up on the railing. When he spotted us, he swung his feet down onto the floor with a thud and stood up, looking down at us from the porch.

"Hey, Spencer," he said casually as if they hung out regularly. "What's up?"

We crossed into the yard. I watched Spencer's Adam's apple bob as he swallowed. "My brother said you took his lottery ticket. I came to get it back."

"Oh, you mean this?" Archie pulled my scratcher out of his shirt pocket, pinching it between two fingers. "He gave it to me."

"You grabbed it out of my hand!" I shouted.

Archie frowned. "I don't know what he's talking

about. He gave me this ticket and when I scratched it off, I saw that I had won." He fanned the ticket in the air.

His utter bold-faced lying made me speechless. I couldn't believe his nerve. I felt like I was tied in knots but about to explode.

"Archie, give it back to him," Spencer said. His voice was weary, like he had already given up.

Archie just smirked. "Why would anybody give away three thousand dollars? You're not making much sense, man."

Spencer turned to me. "Enly, knock on the door. We'll talk to his mom."

I threw him a look. We both knew from Randy's phone call that Archie's parents weren't home. But Spencer just thrust out his chin for me to go ahead.

"You're going to tell my mommy? Ha! Why would *my* mother believe you over me? Besides, she's not even here."

I glanced at Spencer again, wondering what he was up to. He jutted his head at me impatiently like Mom always did when she was waiting for me to do as I was told.

I climbed the four stairs to the door, feeling Archie's eyes on my back. I was raising my hand to knock when, from the corner of my eye, I saw a streak of movement.

Spencer was dashing forward. He grabbed the porch rail near Archie, pulled himself up, and seized the ticket from Archie's fingers. Then he dropped back down to the lawn and started running.

Archie was stunned for just a second before he let out a garbled yelp, swung himself over the railing, and pounded after Spencer. Spencer was fast, but not fast enough. Archie caught him by the shirt by the time he reached the sidewalk and swung him back around into the yard. Spencer hit the ground. His glasses flew off just before his face smacked the dirt. He was struggling to get on his feet while wildly trying to break free, but Archie still had him by the shirt. He got a grip on Spencer's arm, and that's when I woke up.

I sprang off the porch, charged across the lawn, and barreled straight at Archie.

We both slammed onto the grass, me on top of Archie. He must've lost his grasp on Spencer, because the next thing I knew Spencer was pushing on his glasses and dragging me to my feet.

"Let's go!" he shouted.

18

We ran and ran and ran. I somehow still had my melodica on my shoulder, and it banged against me with every step. I was struggling to keep up, and we'd gone four or five blocks before I realized that we weren't headed in the direction of our house.

"Where are we going?" I yelled. "This isn't the way home!" I dropped to a limping walk.

Spencer glanced back, looking past me down the street as if he was checking that Archie wasn't chasing us. Only then did he slow down.

"We're going to Golden Years," he said when I caught up.

Golden Years. Mom's workplace. A squawk of protest escaped me. He was going to tell Mom about the ticket! "Wait! Wait a minute!"

"Are you serious? After all that?" He glanced

over my head again.

I looked back too. No one there.

"We need to get Mom to sign the ticket before Archie shows up looking for it." Spencer seemed to realize he was still holding the ticket and quickly slid it into his pocket.

"But you know Mom won't let me keep the money!"

He let out an exasperated sigh and shrugged one shoulder as if he knew this was true, but sorry, too bad. "What other choice do we have?"

"Can't we find someone else to cash it for us?" I said.

Spencer gave me bug eyes like I was asking him what would happen if I licked my finger and stuck it in a socket. "Really, Enly? You want to take the chance of losing the money? *Again?*"

"But I'll be losing it if Mom gets it!" I needed an alternative. "I know—what about Pinky's mom?" I'd rejected this idea when Pinky had suggested it, but I had to buy time until I could think of something else. I cringed, remembering my fight with Pinky. It was probably the biggest one we ever had. I didn't know if she was going to let it go, but I'd have to worry about that later.

Spencer made a face. "She wouldn't keep a secret like that from Mom."

I knew he was right, but there had to be some way. "We'll tell Pinky's mom that it's Pinky's ticket. And Pinky will say she wants to use the money to pay for my camp!" I wanted to forget about our argument and just think about the Pinky who wanted to help me. After all, music camp had been all her idea.

Spencer scoffed. "That would never work. Who would let their kid give away three thousand dollars to another kid?"

"Mom would," I said glumly. "She'll *let* me give it to you!"

"You know what I mean. Come on, let's go!" He was antsy.

"Wait a minute. Just let me think." I hustled to keep pace with him. "What about Ms. Maisie? I bet she'd do it."

Spencer didn't even slow down.

"Ms. Maisie loves music," I said. "She knows what this music camp means to me! She said she wished she could help me get there."

He shook his head. "It's not going to work. We're going to Mom."

"No, we are not!" I stopped walking.

But Spencer didn't stop. He was getting farther and farther away.

"Spencer!" My mind spun in all directions trying to think of how to stop him, how to change his mind. "Why won't you help me? You know Dad wouldn't quit!"

It didn't work this time. He was giving up, he was going to give the ticket to Mom. Band and Jam wasn't going to happen and the winning scratcher in his pocket, my scratcher, was going to turn into money that stayed in his pocket.

"You just want to give it to Mom because you know she'll use the money for you!" I yelled at his back. He didn't turn around, but his head swung from side to side. I ran to catch up to him again, dizzy with desperation and burning up that he was dismissing me.

"She's going to give it to you, the perfect son." I was saying whatever popped into my head. "And you're glad! You just want to keep the money for yourself so you can run off to college."

That made him stop. He turned to face me. "Oh, please! You know what, Enly? This is getting old."

"Well, it's true, isn't it? You'll do anything to get to precious college!"

Spencer sighed. "You're acting like a spoiled brat, Enly—having a tantrum when you don't get your way."

"Spoiled! Ha! I've never been spoiled a day in my life." He knew that more than anyone. "And what's that word for guys like you? Brown-noser?"

His eyes narrowed behind his glasses. "Tantrums are not the way to get people to help you."

"No, wait—freeloader! That's it. You're a money-grubbing freeloader!" I knew I was being ugly, but for some reason I couldn't quit.

"Grow up!" Spencer shook his head. "It's just music camp. You never even heard about it until three days ago!"

Just music camp. Why was what I wanted a *just*? Maybe what I wanted wasn't as easy, sensible, or prestigious as what everyone else did or thought I should do. But why couldn't I have what I wanted *just* once? Especially when it was right there. Right there, so close. It infuriated me that he couldn't see it. Refused to see it.

"Three thousand dollars would pay for a lot, right? In case you don't get any scholarships." I spat out the words, hitting him where he was sensitive. Mom constantly talked about how Spencer had to get a scholarship. And even though colleges probably were going to fall all over themselves to give him money, I knew he worried about it, and that was why he was always studying so hard and working so much.

Spencer stared at me with a cold look. His face was smudged with dirt from where he had hit the ground when Archie tackled him. A bruise was beginning to show.

I bit my lips. My head was still buzzing from being worked up, but I was already beginning to regret what I'd said.

Spencer pulled the scratcher out of his pocket and held it up in front of my face. I reached for it, but he opened his hand and the scratcher fluttered to the sidewalk. I bent down to grab it, and when I straightened up all I saw was Spencer's backside as he strode away from me.

19

The scratcher was safe in my hand, and I was pretty sure Spencer wasn't going to tell Mom about it, but I felt pretty crummy about losing my temper and saying all those things. I supposed it *was* sort of a tantrum.

I wasn't sure what to do now. My stomach grumbled, partly because it was past dinnertime and partly because of my awful little explosion. I wanted to go home, but I didn't want to face Spencer. I knew I had to apologize, but it was better to let him cool down first.

I started back toward downtown, trying to push down my bad feelings. What Spencer said about Archie coming after the ticket had me paranoid, and I found myself peering over my shoulder all the way to the Olmstead Apartments. I shoved the scratcher deep into the back pocket of my jeans.

Inside the Olmstead, I looked at the mailboxes on the wall to one side of the entry doors to find Ms. Maisie's apartment number. She lived on the third floor. When I knocked on her door, she took a long time to answer.

"Enly! What are you doing here?" She was wearing a thick burgundy robe that matched her burgundy hair, currently rolled in pink foam curlers. Over Ms. Maisie's shoulder I could see that the blankets of her bed were pulled back and mussed as if she had gotten out of bed to answer the door. The TV blared in the background.

"Hi, Ms. Maisie. I'm sorry to bother you, but I need to ask you something."

"Come on in, sweetie! Does your mom know you're out so late?" The clock near her kitchenette showed 6:38. It wasn't even totally dark yet.

"Mom's still at work," I said, evading the question as I followed her inside.

Ms. Maisie put her hand on a dresser next to the door to steady herself, then reached out to the footboard of the bed, sort of furniture-surfing across the room. Her four-wheeled walker was next to the door, but she obviously wasn't using it because of the close quarters. On the other side of the bed was a table near the kitchenette, which held a sink, a small fridge, and a two-burner stove in an alcove along one wall. It was even smaller than our kitchen.

Ms. Maisie snapped off the television and slowly lowered herself into one of the chairs at the table, gesturing for me to take the other one. I took the melodica off my shoulder and placed it on my lap as I sat.

"Now what is it that you need to ask? I see you've got your new instrument there. Did you forget part of our song?"

"No, I'm doing okay with the song, but you know how I've been busking for camp money? Well, someone dropped a lottery ticket into my tip box." I pulled it out, showed it to her, and explained how I needed help with cashing the ticket. I left out all the stuff about getting tricked, getting the ticket back, and fighting with Spencer, but because I knew she'd want to know why Mom couldn't just cash it for me, I went ahead and told her why I didn't want to turn it over to her. What Spencer had said about all of this getting old—meaning I was whining out the same old story—was in the front of my mind, so I made the *poor me* part as short as I could.

"So, I'm looking for an adult I can trust who can

go to Raleigh and bring back the money," I said, topping off my story.

"Raleigh? Oh dear." Ms. Maisie pressed a hand to her cheek. "But you know I don't have a car. I don't even drive for that matter."

"The bus station is just two blocks away," I said.

"That's the city bus station." Her eyes drifted off into the middle distance as if she was thinking, and hope began to bubble in my chest. "I'd have to walk all that way, get on the city bus to the Greyhound bus station over on the east side of town, get off the bus, get on another . . ." The lines around her eyes began to deepen in her wrinkled face, and her eyes flicked to her walker.

I winced, immediately realizing what a terrible idea this was. Ms. Maisie's eyes were bad. She wasn't very mobile. All that walking to the bus station would be like climbing a mountain for her.

"Oh Enly, I do so want to help you, but . . ."

"Maybe you could take a taxi to the Greyhound bus station?" I felt sort of smarmy suggesting it, but I couldn't just give up after everything I'd gone through to get the scratcher back.

"That's certainly a possibility. Only, taxis are quite expensive. The fare, I mean—and I'd have to pay for both ways. And the bus tickets to and from Raleigh, and another taxi to get to the lottery office. All that would cost, and you know I'm on a fixed budget."

"I would pay for it, of course!" I did a quick calculation of what I had left after buying the melodica, plus $5.82 from tips—actually more than that, since in the excitement over the scratcher win, Pinky and I hadn't done a final count before we rushed off to the drugstore. "How much do you think it would cost?"

"Hmm, I don't know. About twenty dollars for each taxi ride? We'd have to do some research for the bus ticket to Raleigh. Maybe fifty, sixty dollars each way?"

One hundred and sixty dollars. "I don't have that much," I admitted.

Ms. Maisie tilted her head at me sympathetically, and we sat in silence as the bubbles of hope in my chest went *pop-pop-pop*. I began to pick at the rolled trim of my melodica case. If I wanted to go to camp, I was back to where I'd started. I'd have to earn all that money.

Or would I?

"Wait. I just thought of something!" I held up my melodica case. "I can busk for the bus fare!"

I wondered how long it would take to make $160 dollars. A lot less time than earning $2,800. I could just sit on the scratcher until I earned the travel money. As long as Spencer didn't mention the ticket to Mom.

That foul churning of my stomach started up again as those terrible things I'd said to him came back to me. Would he tell her? Normally, I wouldn't have thought so, but I'd been such a jerk.

I'd worry about it later, because another thought jumped into my head. "Oh, and Ms. Maisie, we only have to get the money for one direction, because you can pay for the return trip out of the lottery money!"

"Oh, that's good thinking, Enly!" Ms. Maisie patted my hand. "Very good thinking! Now you start working on making that eighty dollars, and I'll work on getting my nerve up and this old body in shape for that long, long trip." She rocked back and forth three times before she got enough momentum to get on her feet, then stood swaying a moment before she started moving toward the door.

Although I should have been thrilled that Ms. Maisie was going to help me, I left her apartment with an uneasy feeling, picturing her trying to get up and down the big steps of the buses and walking across a couple of bus stations by herself. After all, I was her errand boy specifically because she had so much trouble getting around. Not only that, but the trip would take an entire day, and here she was going to bed at 6:38 p.m. on a regular day.

But as she stood in the door, waving and smiling as I headed to the elevator, I thought, who was I to doubt her? If she was determined to help me, I had to let her. Didn't I?

20

Outside the Olmstead, the evening was beginning to dusk up, the sky gray and pink with floaty clouds. The streetlights were on and the shops' windows glowed. The tourists were out in full force, going in and out of the restaurants, shops, and galleries, which stayed open late on the weekends. I wove through them, looking for a good spot to pull out my melodica.

I figured I had about an hour to beat Mom home, and I was sure I could make a good dent in the money I needed for Ms. Maisie's trip. The crowd clotted up near Wedge Park, a small triangular plaza at a crossing of three streets with a few trees sprinkled around. Dozens and dozens of people were beating on hand drums of all sizes in the weekly Saturday night drum circle. People were dancing, hopping and skipping around, swinging their arms wildly. The noise was so loud and the crowd was so thick that a busker couldn't compete with it. I skirted around the edge of the mob, and that's when I almost bumped into Archie coming out of Taco Mamas.

I spun around and dove into the crowd. People scowled and jabbed me with their elbows as they swayed on their feet and bounced in time to the battering of all the drums.

I almost made it to the other side of the park before Archie was suddenly next to me. He hooked my arm and shouted something. I couldn't quite hear what he said, but I was pretty sure it was something like, "Give me that ticket, or else!"

I tried to jerk away, but he held me tight. For a second I thought about yelling or making a scene, but because of the crush and the party mood, no one would take any notice, or if they did they'd just think I was dancing and letting loose. Instead, I sagged out a heavy breath and drew out the ticket that was in the front pocket of my jeans. The green gold of it flashed under the overhead streetlight as I held it up.

Archie's eyes glinted as he reached up to take it. But instead of letting him have it, I flung it past his head. He cursed and his face twisted with anger, but he let me go and plunged into the crowd, scrambling after the ticket.

I didn't wait around and pushed through the spectators and tourists streaming toward the drum circle. Only when I was at least half a block away did I dare to glance back. Archie was holding the scratcher up to the light of his phone.

Darn it! He wasn't going to fall for it!

I had tossed him one of the other scratchers I still had in my pocket, hoping that he'd take the decoy home and let me go. But he was checking it. He wasn't as much of a dingleberry as I thought.

Now Archie's head was straining over the crowd, searching. He spotted me.

I scooted up the street, thinking I'd go around the block and run home. Luckily, the traffic was terrible enough in town that the cars weren't going anywhere. Even when the lights were green, the cars were either hardly moving or at a full standstill, and I could jay-walk without killing myself. But when I glanced back again, I could make out Archie shoving past the slow-moving tourists, getting closer and closer.

Then, over the hum of idling cars, distant drums, and people on the sidewalk, I heard the low wail of a saxophone.

Saxophone Joe!

I pivoted around with my ears up like satellite dishes, trying to locate him. The foot traffic wasn't as heavy here, and I glimpsed the golden saxophone glinting just outside Lichtenberger's Pawn and Loan. I made my way toward the store, stepping into the street to dodge the pedestrians on the sidewalk, and threw myself down next to Saxophone Joe's wheelchair. Then I pulled my knees up in a huddle and tried to make myself as small as possible.

Saxophone Joe didn't even miss a beat of the melody he was playing, though he raised an eyebrow at me before he turned back to the street.

Before he finished his piece, Archie swept right past us. I hunkered down even smaller, trying to make myself invisible, hoping to hide my face from the light spilling onto the sidewalk through Lichtenberger's window. Abruptly Archie stopped on the sidewalk. His head swung left and right like he was looking for me, and I knew he had lost me. Keeping an eye on him, I sidled up and started to move around to the other side of Saxophone Joe's wheelchair, but just at that moment, Archie turned around.

"There you are!" he shouted.

I tried to run, but I tripped over the single leg-rest of Saxophone Joe's wheelchair and fell against his saxophone case. His tips spilled out onto the sidewalk. The yowl of the saxophone broke off.

Archie was looming over me. "Where is it, stinkbug?"

I flipped over and crabbed backward to get out from under his hulking shadow.

"You need to hand over that lottery ticket." Archie bent down and poked me in the chest, pinning me down on the sidewalk.

"Whoa, whoa, whoa!" Saxophone Joe said. "Now wait a moment, gentlemen. I think you fellas have made a mess of my property, and I need you to take a minute and gather up my earnings before this conversation goes any further."

Archie straightened and took a step back. His face was still mean, but he squinted down at the sidewalk and began kicking a few coins and bills toward me. I gathered them up, chucked them back into the case, and repositioned the case near Saxophone Joe's wheelchair, in the space where his left foot would've been had he still had it. I jumped up and pressed close to his wheelchair.

"That's better," Saxophone Joe said. "Now, then, what's this all about?"

Archie's finger was back, pointing at me. "This dirty thief stole a lottery ticket from me! It was worth three thousand dollars."

"You're lying! It's my ticket. You know it!"

"You handed me that ticket."

"You took it out of my hand!" I sputtered. "You lied and said you were eighteen and could cash it for me!"

"You're the liar!" Archie turned again to Saxophone Joe. "That was my ticket, and this overgrown runt and his brother came over to my house, tackled me, and stole it. Look at what they did to my shirt." Archie twisted around and showed where the seam had ripped on the side.

Saxophone Joe turned his eyes on me, waiting to hear what I had to say.

My head was about to explode with anger. He was mixing the truth with lies, working on Saxophone Joe to side with him. "That's not true. I earned that ticket busking." I was half-whining, half-pleading with Saxophone Joe to understand. "A little girl and her mother dropped that ticket in my tip box!"

Archie scoffed. "Who drops a lottery ticket into a tip jar?"

"You'd be surprised. You really, really would." Saxophone Joe closed his eyes in a long blink and swung his head side to side. "But now it really isn't my place to resolve this sort of conflict." He raised his arm and knocked on the glass of Lichtenberger's store window.

In a moment, Mr. Lichtenberger popped his shiny shaved head out the door. "Hey, Joe. How's it going? What's going on?"

"Oh, it's not too bad. We got a serious disagreement here that needs mediation. How about you call the APD and ask them to send one of their finest over this way?" He twitched his mouth to the left and right, then ticked his head forward.

The Altamont Police Department!

"Yeah! Please, Mr. Lichtenberger! Ask for Officer K. Petty!" I shot a look of triumph at Archie. "I've already reported you to the police! Officer Petty knows all about what happened." Oh, I was on a roll now. Although I hadn't put in an official report, the fact that Officer Petty knew the story surely had to be worth more than anything Archie could say.

Archie knew it too. As Mr. Lichtenberger ducked back into the store, Archie narrowed his eyes at me. I just gave him a big, tight smile to show that I wasn't scared. And that I wasn't bluffing either.

I clasped my hands together in front of me. My hands itched to dive into my back pocket and clutch the winning scratcher tucked back there, but I was afraid that if I did, Archie would make a grab for it. "Besides, my mom's already signed the ticket and she has it with her at work." Now *this* was a bluff, but I thought it would give me an extra bit of insurance.

Archie's mouth pinched up. "I'm going to get you for this." He started stepping backward as if to leave, still looking at me with snake eyes.

"Nah! Now, don't be talking like that," Saxophone Joe said to him. "No one's going to be getting anyone! Shoot, if anything were to happen to this boy, that police report with Officer K. Petty and all the brawling I witnessed here on the sidewalk will really come back to bite you."

Archie huffed and rolled his eyes as if he didn't believe any of it. But I could tell he was just making a show of it, because he spun on his heel and stalked away.

I let out a great big shaky breath.

21

Saxophone Joe and I watched Archie disappear into the crowd on the sidewalk. "So you really got a ticket worth three thousand dollars?" Saxophone Joe asked.

"Yep!" I pulled it out of my back pocket and showed it to him.

He chuckled. "I thought you said your mama had hold of it."

"I didn't want Archie to think he could get it off me!"

"Well, you better run yourself home and get your mama's John Hancock on it before you do lose it."

I re-pocketed the ticket and pulled my melodica case around from my back, where it was miraculously still hanging from my shoulder, though it had come partly unzipped. "Actually, I want to busk for a little while." Now that I knew Archie wasn't going to bug me, I thought I should take advantage of the big Saturday evening crowds before I had to get home. "I need to make some money." I unzipped the case while I explained how Ms. Maisie was going to cash the ticket for me.

Saxophone Joe listened with his eyebrows staying high up on his forehead. When I was done he said, "That sure is a lot to go through to get that lottery money. Kind of risky, don't you think, holding on to it like that?"

I couldn't agree or disagree, because I realized I couldn't find either of my instrument's mouthpieces—the small one or the one with the flexible tube. I scoured the sidewalk around us, thinking they had probably fallen out.

"You lost something?" Saxophone Joe asked.

"Yes, the mouthpieces to my melodica." The case had been partway unzipped when I took out the melodica, though I didn't know how long it'd been like that. "Oh no! What if I lost them on the way here? They could be anywhere between here and . . . ugh!" Archie's house. Maybe even still in his yard after we had tussled.

I dropped down to a squat against the building.

My melodica was useless. "How am I going to make the money for Ms. Maisie to get to Raleigh?" I tapped a key on the melodica. The absence of sound made me feel so hollow.

"Mm, mm, mm." Saxophone Joe cocked his head and clicked his tongue. "That is a terrible shame."

"I wonder if Mr. Lichtenberger sells any mouthpieces in the Pawn and Loan." I jumped up. "I'm going to check."

The door chimed as I pushed through. Mr. Lichtenberger looked up from where he was behind the jewelry case arranging some watches. "Everything all right out there?"

"Yes. I guess we'd better call off the police. We worked it out by ourselves. Or at least with Saxophone Joe's help."

Mr. Lichtenberger waved his hand. "No worry about that. I didn't even ring them up. Joe and I have a signal and our own special procedure for working with troublemakers." He shifted his lips to the left and right and cocked his head down, the same motions Saxophone Joe had made, only ending with a big grin. "Is there something else you need?"

I held up my melodica, explained about the lost mouthpieces, and asked if he had any in stock.

"Sorry—I don't generally get many melodicas, so I don't carry any spare parts."

I sighed. "Just thought I'd ask. Thanks anyway."

"I'll bet you can order them online," Mr. Lichtenberger suggested as I was going out the door. "Should only cost a few dollars."

"Oh, okay. Thanks again."

Back outside, I bent over to pick up the case and started putting away the instrument.

"No luck on the mouthpieces?" Saxophone Joe asked.

I shook my head. "I guess I'll have to order them. Which unfortunately means asking my mom to help." I couldn't tell her how urgent this was. She'd probably take forever to get around to placing the order. "Do you think Mr. Lichtenberger could order them through the shop?" Even if I had to pay extra, it might be worth it to avoid having to ask Mom.

"You know what I think?" Saxophone Joe said.

"What?"

"I think you should call it a day. Go on home to your mama, show her that ticket, and leave it up to her as to what to do with it."

I frowned. "But I *know* what she's going to do with it."

"Maybe you do, maybe you don't." One side of his mouth went up with a wry smile. "I know you got this all-fire determination to make this travel money, get that three thousand bucks, go to this camp and be some hot musician, but do you really want to take any more chance of losing that ticket? You already lost it once, and now you lost pieces of your instrument." He narrowed his eyes at me. "How many days is it going to take to make Ms. Maisie's travel money?"

I felt the *But, but . . . I can do it* argument frothing up inside me.

"And truth is," Saxophone Joe continued, "I know Ms. Maisie wants to help you, but she ain't been farther than the doctor's office in years. And when she goes, she's chauffeured there by Mountain Medical Transportation. How long has it been since she's even been down to the pharmacy?"

My heart sank. I knew what he was saying was true. The trip to Raleigh would be too much for Ms. Maisie, and I shouldn't have asked her. My ears were hot again, this time from shame. I had talked myself into believing that Ms. Maisie really could make the trip to Raleigh because she wanted to help me.

Just like Spencer had wanted to help. And Pinky

too. Another wave of guilt came over me as I remembered the rotten things I had said to both of them.

Saxophone Joe leaned over and patted the melodica in its case. "I know you don't want to hear this, but you got a mama and a brother, and you got to trust them to do right by you. Who knows? There's always the chance that your mama will surprise you."

There's always the chance. What Dad used to say.

"And if not, well, she's your mama, and you're a kid, and you got plenty of time to learn the music."

22

The streetlights spilled pools of light on the sidewalk as I crossed under the overpass back into the neighborhood. I trudged home with a heavy heart. I dreaded having to turn over the scratcher to Mom after everything I'd gone through—not to mention that I would have to face Spencer. I felt bad for what I had said about his wanting to keep the money for himself. I knew it wasn't fair, but I couldn't help resenting him, because—despite what Saxophone Joe said—I had a hard time believing there was any chance Mom wouldn't confiscate the money for his college fund.

Spencer was on the couch watching videos on his school laptop.

"Hi," I said.

He didn't look up and his mouth stayed set.

"Eat yet?" I asked.

He ignored me.

"I'm going to make some noodles. Want some?" I said.

Still nothing.

I went straight to Mom's secret stash of ramen and started boiling the water for it. She'd be home in about fifteen minutes, but I didn't care if she caught me. I was sure she'd be so distracted by the lottery win that she wouldn't even care.

While I waited for the noodles to cook, I finally said to Spencer, "Look, I'm sorry about what I said earlier."

He didn't turn around or nod his head, just kept looking at the screen. He wasn't going to get over it so easily.

"I know you tried to help," I said to the back of his head. "I was just mad that Mom . . . you know. It's just that you're always . . . Well, everyone always listens to you."

Apologies were hard. Spencer and I didn't normally have fights like this, so I wasn't really used to talking through why I'd gotten in such a knot and acted like such a jerk. I didn't know what else to say. I knew it wasn't enough, but the noodles began to boil over, and I got busy with adding the seasoning packets and egg, then burning my tongue as I scarfed down the scalding soup. Spencer was still quiet, but the room didn't feel quite so stuffy to me.

I'd finished the noodles and was rinsing out my bowl when Mom got home. She kicked off her shoes at the door, dropped her work bag, and flumped onto the couch.

"You guys just eat?" she asked as Spencer moved over to a chair so she could swing her feet up and stretch out.

"Yes," I said, at least answering for myself.

"Put some tea on for me, will you?" Mom asked.

"Okay."

Mom pulled off her glasses, set them on the coffee table, and laid her arm across her face as she waited for me to make her tea. "What did you guys do today?"

"Work," Spencer said. I knew he wouldn't say anything about the scratcher or the trouble we'd had. Even if he was still mad at me, he wouldn't want to make problems for Mom when she was so tired.

"Did you finish your essay, Enly?"

"Pinky and I worked on a school project," I said. "And I busked a little."

"Did you make any money?"

Spencer lifted his eyes from his laptop.

"Um, yeah, about ten or twelve dollars." I guessed at my tip total. "And this lottery ticket worth three thousand dollars."

Mom raised her head and looked over to me. "What?" But just as quickly, she dropped her head back onto the cushion. "Oh! You're kidding me."

"No, Mom, look." I pulled the ticket out of my pocket, crossed to the couch, and handed it to her. She grabbed her glasses and studied the scratcher for several moments. I grinned at Spencer. He smirked as if to say, *It's about time.* I knew he had forgiven me.

"It's one of those gag tickets, isn't it?" She squinted at me suspiciously. "You can't fool me. Why would anyone give you three thousand dollars?"

"No, it's real. A girl and her mom came out of the drugstore with a bunch of them and put three of them in my tip box. They hadn't scratched them."

Mom didn't seem to hear me. She had turned the card over and was examining the fine print on the back.

I hunted in the junk on the coffee table until I found a pen and thrust it at her. "We have to go to

Raleigh to cash it, but sign it now so no one else can claim it."

Mom took the pen from me automatically, but her mouth was open like reality hadn't sunk in yet. It was kind of fun to see her speechless like that. Still, I was impatient for her to make it ours.

"Sign it, Mom!"

She swung herself upright and signed the ticket on the coffee table. Once she placed the pen down beside it, she sat back staring at the card before she looked at me. "Really?"

I nodded.

Mom's eyes got really big. She started laughing, instantly filled back up with energy. She reached over, pulled me to her, and squeezed. "You got this by busking? I can't believe it! I just can't believe it." She rocked back, dragging me across her lap and smooching me all over my face and head. "It's just amazing!"

I squirmed out from under her wet kisses, trying to move off her lap, but inwardly I was pretty pleased with myself. Her arms finally loosened and I scooted over to my own cushion.

That's when she leaned forward again and clapped Spencer on the knee. "Spencer! Three thousand dollars! That's a big dent into your first year's tuition! What do you think of your brother?"

Just like that.

I knew it.

A look passed between Spencer and me. My look said, *I told you so*, but I couldn't say anything out loud because a huge lump had moved into my throat.

"Mom, that Enly's money," Spencer said. "I don't want it."

Mom beamed at me but she spoke to Spencer. "Enly understands we need this money for college next year. He knows how hard we've been trying to make sure you get there. He wants to help, right, Enly?"

"I don't need his help," Spencer said before I had to answer.

"Sure, sure." Mom waved her hand. "You'll get a scholarship or financial aid, but there're so many other expenses beyond tuition."

"Mom—" Spencer tried.

"Don't argue! We're family, and we help each other. You'll be working by the time Enly's ready for college and you'll help pay for him. He doesn't need this money now. Right, Enly?"

I picked at the fraying cloth of the couch. Mom

was pulling the *We All Help Each Other* card. I knew I should get on board, especially when Spencer had tried to help me and was still trying to help me after I had been a jerk to him. But Band and Jam was calling me. And I was sure Spencer would be fine without my money.

I drew in a big breath. "Actually, Mom, I was hoping to go to that music camp I told you about. Remember? Band and Jam."

She looked confused for a moment before she remembered. "Oh, that!" She frowned. "No."

"But Mom, you said we couldn't afford it. But the money's right here now! What do you call it when it just comes to us? A windfall."

"Enly! This may be a windfall, but we can't spend it on something like camp when we have four years of college to pay for. You know how long it would take me to save three thousand dollars? Maybe three years working like I do now. And once your brother starts college, I'm sure I won't be able to save anything." She sighed. "I wish I had finished college, I wish I had a better job. I wish . . ."

She trailed off, and I figured that last wish was about Dad.

"I don't like for you kids to have to go without,

but I don't want you to struggle like I do when you get older. Look how hard your brother is working even now to get to college—his part-time job after school, homework, applying for every scholarship. You know it has to be this way when money comes to us!"

Mom patted my leg before she got up to put the ticket into her wallet. "I'll try to get Monday off to cash the ticket. Meanwhile, Enly, what about that essay your English teacher wanted you to write?"

The teakettle started shrieking. I just stared at the worn spot on the couch. I could feel Spencer's eyes on me, but I didn't look up. It had happened just like I knew it would. All those feelings of guilt I'd had earlier were wiped away. I felt like screaming that it was unfair, pitching a fit, throwing things, but I knew it wouldn't do any good.

Mom was in the kitchen humming to herself as she finished making her tea, totally oblivious to my misery. "Hey," she said, holding up the empty foil package, "who's been eating my ramen?"

I got up, went to the bedroom, and slammed the door behind me.

23

Mom went to work on Sunday. She left a note saying that she had found someone to swap days with her so she could go to Raleigh on Monday. She also left a list of things that needed to get done, with a tiny box drawn next to each one so Spencer and I could check off each chore as we completed it.

Take out trash
Wash dishes
Clean bathroom
Eat three fruits or vegetables by lunchtime
Enly—DO ESSAY

I had promised Spencer I would do all his chores for the rest of the year if he helped me get my scratcher back, but now, since he was going to get my money, there was no way I was going to take on his workload for the next eight months. I grabbed the pencil and ticked off each box, pushing so hard the graphite tip snapped off just as I x'd on *clean bathroom.*

There! Now Spencer would think I had done his chores, and when Mom came home and saw that they weren't done, he'd be the one to get in trouble.

I grubbed around the kitchen, made some cheese toast for a late breakfast, and went to the living room to eat it and watch TV. Spencer came out of the bedroom. His hair was all wild and sticking up. Sunday was the only day he slept late because he didn't have to go to work until eleven thirty.

"Hey," he said.

I ignored him and kept my eyes on the TV.

He moved to the kitchen and got himself a glass of water. From the corner of my eye I saw him pick up Mom's note. He looked at the trash. It was obviously full. I steeled myself to snap at him when he started in about our agreement. But he didn't say anything. Instead he pushed all the garbage down, tied up the bag, and took it outside.

I was still in my chair stewing with resentment when he came back in.

"Mom said for me to make sure that you did your essay before you went out today," he said.

"You don't get to tell me what to do," I muttered.

He stared at me for a moment. I waited. But instead of bossing me or telling me off, he crossed over, turned off the TV, and perched down on the edge of the coffee table.

"Enly, I'm really, really sorry about camp," Spencer said. "I know how much it means to you. It's really not fair."

Ugh! He was going to be nice to me. I shifted my eyes until they landed on a crack in the ceiling near the corner of the room.

"I tried to convince Mom that I won't need your money, but you know how hardheaded she is. Even I, *the perfect son*, couldn't change her mind."

I refused to smile. I wasn't ready to stop being mad and feeling sorry for myself.

"I know you think Mom's being all harsh on you, but just because she doesn't have to ride me doesn't mean I don't feel the pressure. I've been hearing this *college, college, college* thing for a lot longer than you have. You're too young to remember, but after Dad died, things got really bad—Mom all sad, having to work while trying to take care of us, having to move a few times. So of course I got in line with her plan."

Tears were building up behind my eyes. Feeling sorry for myself was getting mixed up with feeling sorry for Mom and Spencer, feeling sad that I hardly remembered Dad.

"I didn't have this other thing to get excited about like you do with music, though," Spencer said. "I promise I'll do whatever I can to help you go to camp next year. The money will still be in the bank next summer, and by then I can try to make Mom see that I don't need it."

He got up and went into the bathroom. I was glad, because I didn't want him to see me swipe away the tears.

Just then I heard a rattle and clank just outside our door. I got up and yanked it open. Pinky spun around from about five steps away. My blue cookie tin was on the concrete step. She had come to drop off my tips and meant to slip away.

"Hi, Pinky," I said.

"Hey." Her voice was flat and she didn't smile. She was wearing a blue checked skirt and a ruffled blouse that looked dressed up.

"You going to church?" I asked.

"Just got back."

"Thanks for bringing back my tips. Can you come in for a minute?" I picked up the cookie tin and moved to the side so she could enter. She stood for a long moment, as if trying to decide, then finally jerked up one shoulder and came in.

I decided I had to get the apology over right away. "Listen, Pinky, I'm sorry about what I said yesterday."

She crossed her arms. "I'm listening."

She wasn't going to make it as easy as Spencer had. "Um, well . . . I guess . . . I shouldn't have said you have everything easy and handed to you."

"That's right, you shouldn't have said that! I can't help it if my parents can give me more than your mom can. I can't do anything to change that! I was trying to do what I could by helping with the busking plan. And when you insisted on flagging down that police officer, I talked to her more than you did! I was *trying*, Enly."

"I know, I know. And I didn't mean to make you feel bad. I just wasn't ready to give up on the scratcher and was bugged out that you didn't seem to think it was as big of a deal as I did, so I . . . I guess I . . ."

"Lashed out at me." Pinky supplied the words.

"Yes, exactly. I know you wanted to help me get to camp."

"And not just as my sidekick."

"Yeah, I know. I'm really sorry." By now I was completely embarrassed about how I'd been acting.

Pinky had always been my biggest fan. She was on my side, and her friendship mattered more than any music camp.

"Apology accepted. And I'm sorry too. You were right that I didn't really see how much work it's going to take to earn the tuition. It *is* a lot of money. But I counted your tips, minus my seed money. You made thirteen dollars and eighty-nine cents in less than two hours!"

Spencer came out of the bathroom. "Hi, Pinky. Enly can't hang out until he's finished writing his essay. Mom said."

"All right." Pinky went to the door. "Come over when you're done with it," she said to me. "We can make a plan."

"I don't know." I sighed. "It's probably not going to happen. It's just too . . . too much."

Pinky opened her mouth as if she was about to launch into a pep talk, but she closed it as her eyes drifted around the apartment like she was seeing it for the first time. I imagined she was really letting it sink in—how much $3,000 was to my family, and that what was easy to come by for some people wasn't so easy for others.

I'd had a similar feeling when I was in Ms.

Maisie's apartment, even though I'd tried to ignore it. As much as $3,000 would've meant to me, it would've made an even bigger difference for plenty of other people. I might not be going to music camp, but I'd also never had to seriously think about skipping a meal—or eating a discarded sandwich off the sidewalk, for that matter. I'd been angry at Pinky for only looking at things from her own perspective, but I had some work to do in that area too.

After a moment, Pinky said, "Well, if not this summer, maybe next?" Her tone was tentative, lacking its usual pluck.

"Yeah, we'll see." I nodded, not because I was feeling optimistic, but because I appreciated that she was seeing the situation for what it was and not trying to blow fluff on everything.

"And in the meantime, we can still hang out today, at least."

"For sure."

After she left, I went to the desk next to the door. Mom had laid out paper and a pencil and the sheet with the essay prompt from school.

Ambitions for the future.

Big sigh.

I moved to my keyboard instead and proceeded to spend the next hour playing all the songs Ms. Maisie had taught me while Spencer cleaned the bathroom, took a shower, and made himself something to eat.

By the time I'd run through all my songs a couple of times, Spencer had to go to work. He stood over my shoulder for a moment. I could feel him behind me. Finally he said, "Do the essay, Enly. Mom will blow up if you don't have it done by the time she gets home." He left.

I glanced at the essay prompt on the desk again. I knew he was right. Mom wasn't going to accept *I didn't get around to it* for an answer. But I couldn't stay in the apartment any longer. I popped the lid off the cookie tin and stuffed all the money into my pocket, then went to the bedroom and got the rest of my Chinese New Year cash.

24

Downtown, the sidewalks were beginning to fill up with people coming out of the restaurants after brunch, which was a thing with the restaurants on Sunday. I walked around and stopped to listen to a guitar player outside of the old Woolworth's department store, which was now a gallery of booths where people sold their handmade wire jewelry, knitted scarves, and pottery. The music reminded me that I had lost my mouthpieces and had no way to play, no way to make any more money. But that didn't matter since I'd given up on music camp.

The pharmacy was just opening up. I went in and loaded up a shopping basket with a ten-pack box of Twinkies, two jars of gherkins, and a couple of packages of string cheese. I also threw in six packets of chicken-flavored instant noodles, the only kind they had. These weren't nearly as good as the ones from the Asian market because they didn't have seasoning packets of flavored oil and red pepper, but I wasn't sure if Ms. Maisie was ready for that level of spice just yet anyway.

At the counter, the sales clerk with the glasses on the chain and the long fingernails recognized me. "Well, looky here. Our big winner!' She began to unload my groceries and peck at the cash register. "Looks like someone is going to have some kind of party."

I gave her a stiff smile, then took my bag and went to the Olmstead.

Piano music floated into the lobby from the family room. The song was "Put on a Happy Face," so I knew it was Ms. Maisie. I went in, set my bag of groceries on the floor, and waited by her walker until she finished.

"Hi, Ms. Maisie."

Ms. Maisie twisted around on the piano bench. "Oh, Enly! What are you doing here? Don't tell me you've already earned my bus fare." She looked alarmed and clutched nervously at the collar of her pink flowered dress.

"No. I just brought you some things." I picked

up the bag and handed it to her. She pulled out the box of Twinkies and her face lit up.

"Enly, you shouldn't be spending money on me," she scolded as she poked into the bag to see what else was there. "We need it for the bus ticket."

"I gave the scratcher to my mom, so you're off the hook, Ms. Maisie. You won't have to go all the way to Raleigh. But I wanted to thank you for wanting to help me."

She looked so relieved that I felt bad all over again that I had asked her in the first place. "But what about the camp? Is your mom going to sign you up?"

I shook my head. "Nah. We have to use the money for Spencer's college. I've given up on the camp."

"Given up? That doesn't sound like you." Ms. Maisie's face puckered up as she opened the box of Twinkies and handed me two in their individual packaging. "Here. Open these up for us so we can have a snack while we think about what to do."

I tore open the Twinkies and bit into mine after handing one to Ms. Maisie. I realized I had never actually eaten one. It was so sweet that my teeth hurt. But in a good way.

"You were so determined to get to that camp," Ms. Maisie fretted as she nibbled delicately on her Twinkie. "I'm sure we can come up with something. What about that busking? That was your original plan, wasn't it? To earn the tuition with your melodica."

"I lost the mouthpieces. Besides, it's just so much money." I sighed and stuffed the rest of the Twinkie in my mouth.

"But you can do it, Enly. I know you can," Ms. Maisie said.

I swallowed hard. "The idea of making almost twenty-eight hundred dollars in tips just seems so . . . exhausting. Unrealistic. Impossible. I've been kidding myself to think I could earn that kind of money."

Ms. Maisie put her hand to her throat and looked shocked, as if I had said a dirty word. "Enly! If your mother heard you talking like that—!"

"Yeah, she'd be thrilled."

"That's not true! No parent wants to hear that their child is giving up on their dreams. And don't forget, I know your mother from when she worked here. You and she are so much alike!"

I made a face at that. "Mom and me? No way."

"Yes, Enly, you're just like her. Determined and hardworking! You're probably mad at your mom right now, but her heart is in the right place. She doesn't want you and your brother to end up struggling like she has. She's determined that you have a better life."

That was almost exactly what Mom had told me yesterday. I wondered if she and Ms. Maisie had talked about this stuff back when Mom worked at the Olmstead, or if Ms. Maisie had just picked up on a lot by reading between the lines.

"I'm sure that if you keep showing her that you're going to keep working for what you want, she won't get in your way."

I half-shrugged. "I don't know. I'm not sure I'm cut out to be a musician anyway."

"Maybe not." Ms. Maisie put up her hands.

I wasn't looking for her to argue with me, but I was just a tiny bit surprised when she said that.

"But I know you wanted to go to this camp to find out if music is something you want to pursue long term. And you want a chance to feel closer to your father." She cocked her burgundy, cotton-candy-puff head at me and smiled. "It's certainly a worthy project to go looking for that connection to him."

I crumpled the Twinkie wrapper in my hand and swallowed a lump that rose in my throat. Even though I didn't have very many memories of Dad, she was right that since this music camp had come up, I'd been thinking a lot about him. But the reality was that I didn't have to go to camp or even play piano to think about him.

Ms. Maisie began to fuss with the plastic bag of groceries on the bench beside her.

"Now, you take the rest of this food right back to the store, get a refund, and buy yourself a new mouthpiece for that melodica." She tied the handles of the bag together in a knot, strained to pick it up, and pushed it at me. "You can earn that money because you have determination, and that is much more important than talent."

I had to take the bag because she just kind of let go, and I didn't want the two jars of tiny pickles to break all over the floor.

"Okay, Ms. Maisie," I said and stood up, but before I left, I lifted the seat of her walker and put the bag into the basket beneath.

25

After everything that had happened the last couple of days, I felt like my hopes and dreams had been put on a roller coaster, then dumped into a leaf grinder and turned into a pile of mulch. From Ms. Maisie's, I went across the street planning to hole up in the library and read classic Donald Duck comics, but I'd forgotten the library was closed on Sundays.

I didn't want to go home yet, so I wandered down Haywood Street. The guitar player was gone from outside the old Woolworth's, and he'd been replaced by an old-time fiddler with a scruffy beard wearing a blue-and-green plaid shirt. I watched from across the street as I thought about what Ms. Maisie had said.

The truth was I didn't really know if I was flat-out determined to be a musician. When Pinky showed me that brochure and said I should come along, she made it sound so simple. I just wanted to go to camp, maybe find out if music was really going to be my thing. When Mom said I couldn't go, the thought of it had sort of taken over. Once I had gotten that scratcher, camp seemed like it was really going to happen. Ms. Maisie said I was determined, but really, I had gotten a little obsessed—entering someone's house, getting into fights with strangers, having arguments with Pinky and Spencer, asking Ms. Maisie to travel despite her health problems. Saxophone Joe hadn't said it, but it had hung there between us—I had been selfish.

And I knew it was important for Spencer to go to college, especially since he—and Mom—had been laser-focused on it for years. I wasn't mad at Mom for holding that money for school. Well, not anymore. She wanted us to have a more secure and comfortable life than we did now, and she was always working to keep things moving in that direction. I'd known this all along, but I'd let myself forget the last couple of days.

"Hey, Jumbo Bones!"

My back went up and I turned to see Tia a few feet down the sidewalk, walking toward me.

"What's that thing you were buskin' with

yesterday, Jumbo?" Although I didn't care for the nickname, she sounded friendly today.

"It's called a melodica," I told her when she stopped to stand beside me.

"A melodica." She tried the word out and bounced her head as if she liked the sound of it. "You're not playing it today?"

"I lost a piece to it."

"That's rough." She shook the iced coffee she was carrying before she took a sip. The tip of the straw was stained bright pink from her lipstick. "Hey, you looked like you were pulling in quite a few dead presidents. How much did you rake in?"

Over three thousand dollars. I sighed inwardly. "Almost fourteen dollars."

"No kidding?" Her head did the impressed bouncing thing again. "Not bad, Jumbo. You were sounding pretty good out there, though you ought to get some new songs."

I tried not to show my amazement that she was being nice to me, even complimenting me. "Yeah, so I've been told—about the songs, that is. But it doesn't matter now. I'm done with busking."

"Really?" She clicked her tongue in disapproval. "If I could play something you can be sure I'd be out here. Can't you get a new part for the piece you lost?"

I shrugged. "Maybe."

"Well, you should look into it. Definitely. You could make some serious bank. I gotta run, see you on the bus!"

"See you." I lifted a hand in a wave, wondering if she was still going to be friendly on the bus tomorrow. It was impossible to guess. Sort of like busking, I supposed. One day you're getting half-noshed subs, the next day bright and shiny lottery tickets.

I turned back to the fiddler across the street. Several people had stopped to watch him. He was dancing now, bringing up his knees and clacking his shoes while still sawing at the fiddle with the bow. His audience nodded along, and when he twanged the song to a stop, everyone clapped.

Ms. Maisie and Tia were right about the busking being a good idea. I had made some decent cash in the less than two hours I had spent out there. Not bad for a beginner.

The fiddler was talking to the crowd, asking if anyone had requests. No one seemed to know what to ask for, but before they could drift away, he said he would play "Sally Ann" and teach everyone how to step dance. He launched into the tune and did a small jig before he broke off the music and pointed to one of the spectators. The guy, caught off guard, actually moved his feet in a pretty good imitation of the steps. Everyone cheered for him, and the fiddler took up the song again, playing it loud and fast while the mood was high.

I couldn't help but grin at the way the fiddler worked the crowd. He really knew what he was doing. I stayed to see how many people dug into their wallets, and I wasn't surprised when almost everyone dropped something into his hat.

Even though I'd given up on camp, a prickle went over me and my hands began to itch. Mom always said if your hands itched, money was coming your way. Or were my hands itching to play?

Maybe it was both. Band and Jam was still four months away. Pretty much the same four months since I had gotten the idea to busk. If I looked at it a certain way, I was not really any worse off than I'd been a few days ago when Pinky first showed me the brochure.

Hadn't Pinky and I done the math and broken it all down—how much time there was, how much I could make each day? It had seemed possible yesterday morning—why not today? Could I really earn almost $2,800?

Maybe, just maybe. I could at least try. I'd have plenty of time once the school year was over.

And if I didn't make enough this summer, there was always next year. For sure I could earn it all by next summer. Like Saxophone Joe said, there was plenty of time to learn the music.

But I had to get Mom to order those mouthpieces.

And to get her to do that, I had to write that essay.

26

Here's what I came up with:

My mother and brother tell me that I'm smart,
but also that I'm lazy. But then they are only
talking about schoolwork, which has to do with
their ambitions and not mine. With schoolwork I
make good grades, even though I don't have to
study a whole bunch. When it comes to music, it's
a completely different thing. I don't have natural
talent, but I love it, and so I practice every
day, run errands in exchange for piano lessons,
spend my birthday money on instruments, and
busk, trying to make money to go to music camp.

I don't know if I'm going to be a famous
musician when I grow up, or even a great but
struggling one like my dad was before he died.

I don't know if I'm going to be an electrical engineer or a doctor like my brother probably will be. And I wish that my mom didn't worry so much about the future, even though I know she has good reasons. I'm only in sixth grade, so my ambitions don't reach as far as my mom's. Right now, I only know that I want to go to Band and Jam Camp, and that I'll busk until I'm blue in the face so I can make it there.

Maybe it wasn't ideal to write that my family believed I could be lazy about schoolwork or that I didn't know what I wanted to be, but those things were true. My English teacher said an essay shouldn't just say what you think the reviewer wants to hear, but that it should be truly self-reflecting and have the sparkle of one's true personality.

I felt pretty good about what I'd written, so when Mom got home that afternoon, I jumped up from the couch, grabbed the paper off the coffee table, and waved it at her.

"I finished the essay!"

She set down her bag, took the sheet of paper from me, and glanced at it. "Looks a little short."

"It's concise. Ms. Libby says an essay should be focused."

"Hmm."

Now that I'd done what she required, I seized the chance to ask her to order the mouthpieces. "So Mom, somehow when I was busking, I lost—"

"Wait!" Mom held her hand up. She moved to a chair and sat down. "I want to read this."

I plopped back down on the couch and clasped my hands together uneasily. She hardly ever looked at any of my homework. Mostly she asked me over and over if I got everything done and checked my report cards to make sure they were all A's. I fidgeted, beginning to feel nervous as her eyes slowly moved back and forth across the page.

I knew she'd gotten to the part about Dad when her eyes got big and suddenly looked wet and filmy. My chest tightened as she put a hand to her face. Her hand stayed there, pressed against her cheek, even after she put the paper down on the coffee table. She didn't say anything, only pressed her lips together and gazed vacantly at the paper on the table.

I could have kicked myself. "Mom, I didn't think you were going to read it. I wouldn't have—"

Mom's hand went up again, and she waved it as if to wipe away anything else I might want to say. "It's a good essay." She nodded at me, her body rocking slightly in the chair. "Very good." She pulled a smile. "Especially when you mention your father."

She blinked a few times like she was trying to keep from tearing up. Then she went to the shelf near the counter that separated the kitchen from the living room and began to poke around. At first I thought she was rushing to organize the books and our old school notebooks to distract herself from memories, but then she pulled out a black-and-white marbled journal and handed it to me.

"What's this?" I asked. The journal was creased, the edges worn from use like the ones we used in school.

She sank back into her chair. "Look."

I opened the journal. Instead of wide-ruled blue lines and heavy pencil scrawls about my summer vacation, this one was printed with staff lines and marked with handwritten musical notes. I flipped through and saw that at least three quarters of the pages were filled with compositions. Some of the pages had just a couple lines, some were heavily smudged with eraser marks, and a few were cleanly scored with pen as if the composer was satisfied with the work and could commit it to ink.

Of course, I couldn't read the music, but a few of the compositions had titles penciled in, like "Is Anyone Out There Listening to This?" and "Just Going for It." When I came to ones called "Spencer" and "Enly" it really sank in that I was looking at Dad's handwriting, his very own music. My chest was bursting and my eyes got super filmy.

"It's for you," Mom said. "Maybe one day you can play them. I like the one called 'Everything's Going to Be All Right.'"

I flipped back until I found it. The actual title was "Everything's Already All Right" but I didn't correct her. I couldn't wait to learn to read music and play it for her.

Mom picked up my essay again and changed the subject. "Now, did Spencer check the grammar yet?"

"Not yet."

She held the paper out to me. "Better give it to him today so you can turn it in tomorrow."

"I will. I'll give it to him right away." I was suddenly so glad that Mom had forced me to write the essay. Not only because of the part about Dad, but because it explained exactly why I wanted to busk.

"But listen, Mom. I lost the mouthpieces to my melodica. I need to get new ones before I can start busking again. Will you help me order them online?"

"How much do they cost?"

"I don't know exactly yet. I'll have to look it up. Probably not very much."

"Okay, but you have to pay me back."

"Yes, of course. I will."

27

I'd been busking for about an hour and a half, but I needed to head home to feed the neighbor's cat. Because it was a Wednesday afternoon and hot as the devil, tips had been slow. I counted what I'd made: $9.75. Not great, but not terrible.

I zipped my melodica into its case and headed back to my street as I did the math in my head. In the last six weeks I'd been busking every chance I got, doing every job I could find, and saving whatever I earned (except for treating Saxophone Joe to tacos one day as a thank-you for all his sound advice). So far I'd saved $261.42. That was a far cry from the $2,800 I needed, but Saxophone Joe said that the tourist season would only increase through the summer. School would be out in a couple more weeks and then I'd be able to busk even more. Mom had almost agreed that I wouldn't have to go to City Rec Camp this year.

At the house, the mailman was cramming envelopes into the six metal boxes on the porch.

"Anything for Number Four?" I asked.

He shuffled some envelopes and flyers, then handed me a stack. I went into the apartment and chucked the mail onto the kitchen counter.

"Is that the mail?" Spencer, on the couch, looked up from his laptop.

"Yep," I said.

"Anything for me?" he asked.

I riffled through them. College catalog, college catalog, bill for Mom, letter for Enly Wu Lewis. What?

I looked at the return address. *Band and Jam Music School*. My heart tripped, but then I realized it must just be a brochure.

"Did I get anything?" Spencer asked again.

I gave him his catalogs, then ripped open my envelope.

Spencer turned back to me. "What's that?"

"Probably another flyer for camp." I pulled out the papers, but there was no brightly colored brochure like the one I kept taped on the wall next to my bed. Instead, there was a thick sheaf of white papers. The first page was a brief formal letter. My eyes sped across the lines.

Dear Enly,

I am pleased to inform you that you have been selected by Band and Jam Music School to receive a full scholarship to the August intensive two-week summer camp. Your video folio and essay have proven that you have the true heart of a musician, and we want to recognize and encourage your continued effort to pursue your dreams.

Enclosed you will find the forms . . .

My heart practically stopped. I scanned the rest of the letter, which was all about the forms that needed filling out. My eyes jumped back to *Dear Enly*, and I started reading all over again. I wasn't sure I had read it right the first time.

"What is it?" Spencer had set down his laptop and was twisted around on the couch, watching me with a strange smile on his face.

I shoved the papers at him. As Spencer read, my mind began to unfog. It began to sink in. I was going to Band and Jam. I was going to music camp!

Spencer whooped. "You got it! Yes!" He came around the couch, grabbed me by the shoulders, and shook me.

My tongue finally started to move. "But . . . but how? How did they know about me?"

Spencer had a proud smirk on his face. "I told you I would help you."

"What do you mean? You did this?" I bent over and grabbed the letter again. *Video folio and essay*, it said.

"Mmm. Kind of." He perched on the back of the couch and crossed his arms. "I sent them that essay Mom made you write, along with some of the video and photos Pinky took of you busking and practicing piano with Ms. Maisie from that neighborhood project. Wrote them a letter."

"And you asked them to give me a scholarship?"

Spencer shrugged like it was no big deal. But it *was* a big deal. A huge deal. The best deal!

I jump-tackled him into a bear hug and we fell onto the couch. Tears of disbelief sprang up and I rubbed them on his shirt. "Thank you! Thank you, Spencer! You're the best brother I ever had. And I'm sorry I ever called you a money-grubbing brown-noser."

"You mean freeloader. Get off me!" Spencer yelped.

I rolled off him. "I have to go tell Pinky!" I shouted. "Ms. Maisie! Saxophone Joe! Mr. Lichtenberger! And Mom! I can tell Mom because she can't give it to you!"

Epilogue

The lights—red, blue, and purple—streamed down on the band and lit the gold banner we had plastered on the wall: The Scratchers!

Pinky shredded out "The Imperial March" on the electric guitar while the drummer drove the beat and I pounded along on the keyboard. My ears, hot with the rush of the moment, roared with the music, the crowd.

I took a deep breath and nodded at our singer standing by. He moved to the front of the stage as I dropped out of the tune, picked up my melodica and stood up. Pinky and the drummer abruptly ceased "The Imperial March," and we all jumped in on "Give My Regards to Broadway," as I rocked forward to the front of the stage.

We sounded terrible, crashing and loud, but

the audience—students, instructors, parents—went wild. The lights were nearly blinding me, but I could still make out Mom and Spencer at the front of the crowd, wincing a little, but also throwing up their arms and hooting, and my heart nearly burst out of my chest.

Author's Note ♪ 𝄞

The day Profa Burdette brought her accordion to the classroom, my then ten-year-old son came home and said he wanted to buy one with his Chinese New Year money so he could start busking. In the past, after listening to coworkers bemoan the burden of their student loan debts, I had occasionally tried to coax my sons into putting their music classes to practical use and making some college tuition money by busking. I was thrilled that Eliot *finally* wanted to try it, so I suggested he ask his piano teacher, Chuck Lichtenberger, where he could purchase a used one. That's when he showed Eliot a melodica and my story radar kicked on.

But aside from busking, lottery tickets, and family connection, Enly's story is also about community. My husband and boys are native sons of our town of Asheville, on which Enly's town of Altamont is loosely based. Having never lived anywhere more than a few years myself until I came to Asheville, I've slowly come to know the richness and complexities of being part of a changing community. This story is a tribute to some of the lovely people and points that make it such an interesting place to live: Isaac Dickson Elementary School, the buskers, the Vanderbilt residents, the neighborhood, Biscuit Perry-Rhoades, Pack librarians, Malaprop's Bookstore, Finkelstein's Pawn Shop, Asheville Discount Pharmacy, and Friday night drum circles.

Unfortunately, as with any *found out* destination, heavy tourism, gentrification, homelessness, and inequity are tricky, painful issues that our community struggles to navigate. Although I only touch on these matters in this book, I hope readers who enjoy Enly's story will also give thought to the lives of ordinary people in their own communities.

Acknowledgments

Exceptional recognition goes to my sons, Alex and Eliot. If I were a more fair and generous person, their names would be on the cover of this novel as coauthors. Besides providing inspiration from their daily lives, they aided in the construction of this story by eagerly asking for pages, making notes in the drafts, vetoing bad material, and scratching quite a few lottery tickets. They were often patient half-listeners to my ramblings about the process and problems of the draft, and although I never really expected them to unsnag the hitches, somehow, amazingly, at the oddest times, they would unexpectedly pull out just the right suggestion when I really needed one.

Forever appreciation to my writing supports: Ann Howell, Linda Steitler, Annice Brown, Williamaye Jones, Shannon Hassan, Amy Fitzgerald, and everyone at Carolrhoda Lab/Lerner. Also thank you to Carolyn Farmer and Nolan Adcock, young beta readers, who gave more gentle feedback than my own kids provided.

Special thanks to Bobbie Joe, who talked to Eliot and me about busking and answered all our questions. The documentary *Buskin' Blues*, directed by Erin Derham and filmed in Asheville, also provided me with further insight into the lives of performers.

Questions for Discussion ♪

1. Why does Enly want to go to music camp so badly?

2. How does Enly's mom express her love for her kids? What things does she do that show how much she cares? How is this similar to or different from the ways you and your family express love?

3. Why do you think Spencer is such a hardworking student and such an obedient son compared to Enly? How has his childhood been different from Enly's?

4. Why does Enly get upset with Pinky? When they argue, are you more on Enly's side or more on Pinky's side?

5. How has Enly's life been harder than Pinky's? What are some ways that he's still been fortunate?

6. Enly's hometown has been changing a lot. What are some changes you've noticed about your town or neighborhood? Do you think they're good, bad, or a little of both—and why?

7. Enly isn't sure that he'll turn out to be a gifted musician. What does he get out of the experience of playing music even if he isn't very good at it?

8. If you ended up with a winning lottery ticket like Enly's, what would you do with the money and why?

About the Author

Jennie Liu is the daughter of Chinese immigrants and a longtime resident of Asheville, North Carolina, where she lives with her husband and two children. She is also the author of the young adult novels *Girls on the Line* and *Like Spilled Water*.